DATE DUE

Aria

of the Sea

by Dia Calhoun

WINSLOW PRESS

Florida ❀ New York

Acknowledgments:
I would like to thank Shawn Zink;
my family, friends, editor, and critique group;
Dr. Mary Simonson for checking the manuscript for medical
accuracy; the Quick Information Reference Librarians of the Tacoma
Public Library for unfailing patience; and the town of Masset
in the Queen Charlotte Islands for inspiration. As always,
I am particularly grateful to Anna, Joan, Chuck, and Rosie
Hommel for the Loft.

Credits:
Untitled poem from *Travelling the Path of Love*, page 54,
edited by Llewellyn Vaughn-Lee, © 1995. Reprinted with permission
from The Golden Sufi Center, Inverness, California.

Calhoun, Dia.
Aria of the Sea / by Dia Calhoun.
p. cm.
Summary: In the magical kingdom of Windward, thirteen-year-old Cerinthe arrives at the Royal Dancing School,
where she finds herself torn between the two careers of dancer or healer.
ISBN 1-890817-25-2
[1. Dance—Fiction. 2. Fantasy.] I. Title.
PZ7.C12747 Ar 2000
[Fic]—dc21 99-462306
Editor: Glenn Pudelka

For Cheryl Gomes
with love still.
And wherever you are,
fair winds be yours.

I am calling to you from afar;
Calling to you since the very beginning of days.
Calling to you across millennia
For aeons of time—
Calling—calling…Since always…
It is part of your being, my voice,
But it comes to you faintly and you only hear it sometimes;
"I don't know," you may say.
But somewhere you know.
"I can't hear," you say, "what is it and where?"
But somewhere you hear, and deep down you know.
For I am that in you which has been always;
I am that in you which will never end.
Even if you say, "Who is calling?"
Even if you think, "Who is that?"
Where will you run? Just tell me.
Can you run away from yourself?

Anonymous
from *Travelling the Path of Love*

Chapter One

The School of the Royal Dancers

Which way? Which way?"
Cerinthe cried, rushing ahead of her father down the crowded
street. "We must find the school soon or I'll miss the Trial. And
we'll have sailed three hundred leagues for nothing!"

"Wait for me," her father called. "Don't get lost in this
cursed city!"

But Cerinthe didn't wait. She dodged a carriage clattering
by on the cobblestones, evaded a peddler who thrust his tray of
shrimp beneath her nose, and then stopped abruptly in the
midst of a flock of sheep being driven to market.

"Watch your way, girl!" A woman in a yellow-and-white
striped dress waved her crook. Cerinthe only stood with her
mouth open, staring across an enormous courtyard. Her father
ran up beside her.

"Could that be the school?" Cerinthe pointed at a

magnificent greystone building. "We've come ten blocks north and twelve west, just as the harbor master told us, but that looks like a palace."

"And how would you know a royal school from a palace?" her father asked, panting. He touched the top of her head. "Until we left home, you'd never seen a dwelling bigger than the village hall."

Cerinthe frowned. How could he jest at such a time? She ducked free of his hand and spotted the words chiseled into the stone across the length of the building.

"The School of the Royal Dancers," she read aloud. "Established by Queen Scallopia of Windward, in the Year Two Hundred of the Royal House of Seaborne." Cerinthe spun on one foot, and her cloak flared. "It is the school. We're here at last!"

All during the voyage across the rough seas of the archipelago, she had both longed for and dreaded this moment. Was it only a month since they had set sail from Normost? Was she truly standing on the royal island of Faranor, the capital of all Windward, looking up at the royal school? She was a dancer, and the royal school offered the finest training in all the kingdom. But would they take her? Was thirteen too old?

"Come on, Father." Cerinthe pulled him into the courtyard. She counted up seven stories to the school's roof, where pointed gables pitched and angled every which way. Lower, in a row across the front, lofty pillars of red-veined marble stood like sentinels.

"Tonea never said," Cerinthe began, her mouth dry. "I

mean…I never dreamed the school would be so—"

"Big?" Her father squinted up. "Aye, it's big enough, all right. Taller than a five-masted clipper would be my guess—and longer than three fields of wheat."

Cerinthe swung her canvas bag. Big was not the word she had been seeking. Grand or rich or splendid—yes, splendid, that was it. Would such a splendid school accept her, a commoner from a fishing village in the far Northern Reach?

A gust of wind skittered across the paving stones. It lifted Cerinthe's cloak, whipping her skirt and the three flannel petticoats that her grandmother, Gwimma, had insisted she wear for the voyage. When Cerinthe pulled her cloak tighter, the brown homespun cloth felt stiff with dirt and sea salt. All of her clothes were blackened with tar from the ship's caulking.

"If only that storm hadn't delayed us," she said. "I wanted to bathe and wash my clothes and rest before the Trial…but just look at me." She touched her greasy hair. "I'm filthy. I smell of herring."

Her father squeezed her shoulder. He looked little better, his leather breeches worn and streaked from hours aloft in the rigging.

"I know," he said. "But, praise Nemaree, we're lucky to be alive at all. As for the Trial, clothes don't matter, clean or otherwise. It's your pretty dancing the teachers want to see."

But Cerinthe, looking anxiously about her as they crossed the courtyard, doubted her father's words. Everything in Faranor seemed not only beautiful but clean and sparkling, too. Towers and domes soared to the north, east, and west, painted in rainbow colors that blurred into the low lying, misty clouds.

"Remember," her father added, "anyone from commoner to princess can come to the Trial—anyone who has what we do. All you need to get through there…" he pointed to the double doors that crowned a sweeping flight of stairs "…is tucked in here." He patted the pocket on his woolen vest.

Inside was the letter from Cerinthe's dancing teacher, Tonea, who had studied at the royal school long ago. Every year, after harvest and before the seas grew wild with winter, the royal school held a Day of Trial. Anyone with a letter like Cerinthe's could come, but only a few would be admitted and trained, and even fewer be offered the chance to join the Royal Dancing Company someday.

Hear me, Sea Maid, Cerinthe prayed to the singing Goddess who rode the waves through all the seas of Windward, who guided the lost and healed the sick. *Please let the royal school accept me. I can't go back to Normost. Not after what happened with Mama.* Cerinthe pressed one hand against her chest, holding back a sudden pain.

She walked faster, toward a rectangular fountain near the bottom of the stairs. Water dribbled over a bronze sculpture of six, no, seven identical dancers posed in arabesques. Although her mouth still felt dry from running, she didn't drink; the pooled water looked brackish, the jets clogged with dead leaves. She fidgeted with her hood, then arranged her bag to hide the biggest stain on her cloak.

"Courage, Daughter!" her father whispered as they climbed the marble stairs. The blue flag of Queen Seaborne and her consort king fluttered to one side. Two white seahorses faced each other on the blue silk; the space between them created a heart. Above the seahorses shone a golden crown, and below, a conch shell. Her Majesty was the school's patron, and all the training was free.

"Where are all the other applicants?" Cerinthe asked, glancing back at the deserted courtyard. "Do you think the Trial is already over? Storm and thunder! What if we missed it? What will I do—"

"Don't go borrowing bad weather," her father said.

At last they reached the double doors. Cerinthe hesitated, then knocked twice. A bald, elderly man in a silver coat with puffed purple sleeves opened the right door.

"Your business?" he asked and raised his spiky, white brows.

"I am Gaebron Gale of Normost," Cerinthe's father said, pulling out the letter. "I have a recommendation for my daughter to attend the Trial. She's the best dancer you'll ever see."

"So says every other parent this side of Skooinos," the doorman said. "And there are but ten places. Besides, the Trial doesn't begin for five hours." He looked Cerinthe up and down. "If she's older than thirteen, they won't try her. Otherwise, show your letter at the servant's door. That's the place for scullions and snippets stinking of fish." With that, he shut the door in their faces.

Cerinthe's cheeks burned. A fierce, proud look flashed in her father's eyes. He was a skilled sailmaker, sought by folk from the forty-four islands of the Northern Reach, and was accustomed to being treated with respect. Still holding the letter, his hand closed into a fist and raised toward the door.

Cerinthe grabbed his arm.

"No," she cried. "Please. Let's go around to the back. I don't care what they say, so long as they let me study here."

"I care," he snapped. "And you ought to. Where's your pride?"

"Mama," Cerinthe said softly. "Mama wanted this, remember? It was the last thing she said before I...before she died."

Slowly, his fist fell. His brown eyes softened, and he sighed.

They walked back down the stairs. The red lines creeping through the marble looked like blood vessels. Cerinthe thrust her hand with its grimy nails deep into her pocket. Only ten places! She had known there would be few—but ten! She might as well go home now. The teachers would never choose her to be a student; she was too dirty, too big, too common.

Buried inside her pocket—beneath her knife, a scallop shell, and a bit of knotted string—was a medallion. Cerinthe jerked her hand away as though her fingers had been scalded. She had forgotten the medallion was there. It was a folk healer's charm, a piece of pottery imprinted with the healer's symbol. Gwimma had slipped it into Cerinthe's pocket just before the ship left. "Dancing is for festivals and moonstruck lovers," Gwimma had scolded. "All that I've taught you so you can be the next healer on Normost wasted. Selfish girl!"

Her father stopped beside the fountain. "Yes, your mama wanted you to study here," he said, tugging on his beard. "She also wanted many other things that I did not: servants, the company of the gentry, and painted paper on the walls. But is this what you want? Do you really want to live here, so far from me and Gwimma? So far from home?"

Cerinthe looked back at the royal school, at the splendid facade, at the tall, forbidding doors that had slammed in her face. Suddenly, she wanted to run to the harbor, jump on the ship, and sail back home to Normost. She wanted her beach and her village, where she knew every creature and every fishing boat, and they knew her. Then she remembered how empty the cottage was without her mother, and her throat ached.

"Well?" her father asked.

"You know I've always dreamed of being a dancer." Cerinthe opened her hand to catch the drops from the fountain, but they were too far away. "I have to try. We've come so far."

"To the back door then," he said, smoothing out the crumpled letter. His shoulders sagged.

The ache throbbed in Cerinthe's throat. She reached into her pocket, grabbed the medallion, and threw it toward the fountain. It arced up, spinning, then smashed against one of the bronze dancers. The pieces sank into the brackish water.

Cerinthe ran after her father and led him toward the back of the school, where the shadow of the gabled building lay like a ragged black scar.

Chapter Two

Daine Ambrose, the dancing master, walked to the front of Crown Hall and announced to the children, "The second stage of the Trial has ended."

Cerinthe, who was still hot from the final jumps, stood sweating in her muslin dancing tunic. Each time she breathed, the paper pinned to her bodice crackled. All the applicants wore their names written in bold letters on a square of paper. Cerinthe smiled down at hers. She had danced well, better than the others, especially during the jumps. A laugh bubbled inside her, and she wanted to start jumping again, higher and higher until she burst through the ceiling into the sky. She felt certain they would choose her.

High on a platform at the front of the hall, a woman dipped a quill in ink and began to write. She sat in a high-backed, carved wooden chair beside a tiny table. The chair's legs curved into the clawed feet of a raptor, half hidden by her long, black skirt. She was Daina Odonna, the head of the royal school and company.

Except for the scratching of the quill, the room was silent. Cerinthe watched the goose feather loop and lift, shaping her fate. At last the daina blotted the page. Cerinthe and the other children who were left in the hall—over two hundred had been dismissed already—let out one long sigh. The daina extended her arm, which was encased in a black sleeve that sharpened to a point on her wrist. She held out a piece of parchment.

Cerinthe stared at it, hope and fear raging inside her. Daine Ambrose took the parchment and turned toward the crowd.

"Marvelous that you all could come," he said. "Wonderful thing. Regrettably, there are only ten places and still fifty of you." He shook his head; his grey hair was as springy as the jumps he had demonstrated. "So we must narrow the number again."

Cerinthe's hand closed and she scratched her nails against her palm.

"In the third stage," the daine continued, "we wish to see fifteen of you dance again before making our final decision. If I call your name, please come to the front. If I don't, change clothes and go directly to the Kestrel Room. The final list of ten will be posted there in?…" He looked toward the platform.

Daina Odonna lifted one finger from the armrest. Her white hair coiled in a bun on her neck, but her face was unlined, her age impossible to guess.

"In one hour," Daine Ambrose said. "And now for the names.

The first is—Leslea Day of Skye." A little blonde girl shrieked and skipped her way to the front. Cerinthe smiled. Daine Ambrose called six more names. Then the eighth. The ninth.

Cerinthe's smile faded. She dug her fingers harder into her palm, closed her eyes, and prayed: *Oh Sea Maid, make him call my name.*

"Jorad Bendour of Stenden Isle," Daine Ambrose called the thirteenth name. "Theadora Windalore of Faranor." He paused. Only one more name. No one breathed. Cerinthe leaned forward. *Please, please…*

"And, finally, Cyril Deane of Trent. That's everyone. Regrettable, regrettable. But thank you. Be sure to wait in the Kestrel Room."

Cerinthe stood stunned. No! she wanted to cry. There's been a mistake! A terrible mistake! Although she had known her chances were slim, she still had hoped—especially when she had danced so well compared to the others.

A thin, curly-haired boy wailed. That broke the spell, and the children began to leave the hall; there was nothing else to do. The fifteen lucky ones, nine girls and six boys, clustered, smiling, around the daine.

Why? Why? Cerinthe fumed as she passed them. She had danced better than Theadora Windalore; she knew she had. The Windalore surname might belong to a family of gentry or might even be a noble name. Cerinthe tore off the paper pinned to her bodice and read it: Cerinthe Gale of Normost. A plain, old, stolid, commoner name. Perhaps Daina Odonna, like the doorman, preferred the upper classes.

Cerinthe glanced toward the platform and saw the daina's

shrewd black eyes watching her. She stiffened, then crumpled the paper and threw it on the floor. Daina Odonna arched one eyebrow while her fingers stroked the blood-red ruby pendant that shone on her breast.

Cerinthe despised her.

Back in the dressing room, women fluttered forward, helping the girls out of their elaborate costumes. One girl, crying in her mother's arms, wore a dress covered with mother-of-pearl buttons that shimmered and shook with every sob. Everyone had someone, everyone, it seemed, but Cerinthe. She took off one slipper, crushed in the heel, and wound the ribbons around the shank.

"I shall try again next year," said a girl with iridescent feathers stitched all over her bodice. "I'm only ten."

Cerinthe took off her other slipper. There would be no next year for her; she would be too old.

"It wasn't a fair Trial," said a plump girl as she wiggled out of a gold brocade skirt. "The combinations were far too long."

Cerinthe struggled with the hooks on her dancing tunic; it felt tight and small. After she yanked the last hook, the tunic slipped from her shoulders, and the white muslin crumpled around her feet. She wanted to kick it across the room. Plain old muslin! Why hadn't Tonea told her to wear a fancy costume? She had danced in muslin among girls dressed like princesses in satin, silk, and lace.

The din of complaints and sobs rose higher and higher. Cerinthe felt as if she had swallowed one of the boulders that crouched in the sea by Dolmar Bluff at home. It sat in her stomach, dragging her down into swirling black depths.

No! She would not cry in front of all these girls. She would not! She was Cerinthe Gale of Normost. She could row five miles against the tide and scoop crabs out of a roiling surf. Sometimes, she could even hear the Sea Maid sing. Cerinthe snatched her tunic off the floor. Her mother had made it, her hope in every stitch. "You are beautiful when you dance, Cerinthe," she used to say. "Like a bird flying on the wind."

Cerinthe folded her tunic and tucked it into her bag. Now she would have to go back to Normost, back to the cottage that felt so empty without her mother. Cerinthe's hands felt stiff, as though they had labored too long in an icy wind. She scowled at them: stupid, stupid hands. It was her fault, all her fault.

She finished dressing. A woman in a lemon-yellow silk dress, festooned with yards and yards of swoops, looked sidelong at Cerinthe's dirty clothes.

"How could your mother let you come to Her Majesty's royal school in such a state?" the woman scolded, a yellow rose quivering on her hat.

"Because she's dead!" Cerinthe exclaimed. "How could yours let you grow up with such rude manners?"

The woman gasped.

With tears in her eyes, Cerinthe picked up her cloak and bag and marched out of the dressing room. I won't go back to Normost, she thought, not ever. I will be a dancer. I will.

She had to find a way.

Chapter Three

Unfair, unjust! Cerinthe walked down the hall toward the Kestrel Room, raging like a storm in the month of Tempestus. A laugh burst from her throat, a laugh that choked into a sob.

Not one of her many fears about the Trial—that she would dance poorly, be late, or misunderstand the teacher's instructions—had come true. She had never thought to fear what *had* come true. She had been prepared to be dismissed if others danced better but not if she did. Was her judgment wrong? Cerinthe rubbed vainly at a stain on her skirt. Maybe her dancing was as shabby as her clothes.

She sighed at the carpet bordered with pink roses. Each rose looked exactly like the next, twining in a row down the hall. The carved ceiling arched high above, painted an icy white, aloof and regal in its grandeur. If only she had passed the Trial, she could have lived here. Never had she imagined a place of such opulence, a place so different from the listing, weather-battered cottages on Normost.

But she had not passed.

How could she convince her father to let her stay in Faranor? "I have nothing more to teach you," Tonea had told Cerinthe before she left. "I only studied at the royal school for a few years." Faranor must have retired dancers who prepared the applicants for Trial and for the lesser dancing companies that toured throughout Windward. But Cerinthe knew such teachers would be expensive. On remote Normost, Tonea had taught her single pupil in exchange for food, but here the teachers would want money. Besides, Cerinthe doubted her father would allow her to live alone in this enormous city.

From the far end of the hall, a maid approached wearing a black taffeta dress and a white linen apron trimmed with lace. She carried a silver tray laden with dishes. When she saw Cerinthe, she blinked rapidly three times, and one of her hands slipped. Silver and china clattered as she caught the tray. Then she rustled past. Cerinthe stared after her, astonished to see a maid wearing finer clothes than anyone on Normost ever wore, even on feast and holy days.

Thordon would never believe her when she told him about this place. Cerinthe walked on, more miserable than ever, wishing she had not thought of him.

She had met Thordon of Tycliff on the *Morning Hope*, the ship that had brought her to Faranor. His eyes were the grey of the sea on a cloudy day. A fisherman's son, he hoped to become an apprentice at the Faranor shipyards. "I have plans, big plans!" Thordon had said, watching her practice on the ship's deck as the shores of strange islands slipped by. They had become friends—maybe more, she hoped, remembering the way he had once held her hand.

Cerinthe looked down at the carpet, her cheeks hot. How could she tell him that the royal school had rejected her? How could she face him, or Tonea, or all the good folk on Normost who had believed in her? She could still see them gathered on the dock to wave goodbye and shout, "Fair winds be yours!" as the *Morning Hope* set sail. And how Gwimma would scold about wasted time and money. Cerinthe bowed her head. At least she would never have to tell her mother that their dream would not come true.

A corridor opened to Cerinthe's left. Over the doorway was a brass sign engraved with the words, *The Gallery of the Great.* Inside, paintings hung on the walls—paintings of dancers! Cerinthe glanced left and right, then walked into the gallery and looked at the first painting, "A Scene from *The Chrysalis.*" Dancers in identical, dun-colored costumes knelt in a line. At one end, a woman struggled inside a rippling swathe of silk, the tip of a wing emerging.

Five minutes passed, then ten, as Cerinthe walked among the paintings and sculptures. She saw Daina Marlina, who had made audiences weep, and Daine Pertol, who had leaped six feet into the air. Tonea had told Cerinthe all about them.

As she approached the end of the hall, where it turned sharply around a corner, Cerinthe knew she should tear herself away; her father would be waiting in the Kestrel Room. Why had Daine Ambrose asked them to wait? Was there a chance that some of the rejected applicants might be on the final list? If not, why couldn't they leave? He had not asked those who had been dismissed after the first stage to wait.

Feeling a glimmer of hope, Cerinthe focused on the sculpture in front of her—the last before the hall turned—and then stood absolutely still. A marble likeness of Daina Kasakol, the greatest dancer in the history of the kingdom, posed on the pedestal. Kasakol balanced on her toe, with one knee bent. Legend said she had been able to turn one hundred fouettés without stopping.

Suddenly, skirts swished; Cerinthe heard people coming down the other hallway. As soon as they turned the corner, they would see her.

"We're alone now, Mother," said a high, petulant voice. The swishing sound stopped. "Tell me what Daina Odonna wrote in her note."

"The usual. You are not applying yourself, Elliana, and she wishes to discuss your behavior. I am weary of these meetings. Do you realize I had to cancel tea with Lady Agard? Why, her dowry could make your brother's fortune!"

"But didn't the daina tell you I'm the best dancer in my class?"

Cerinthe stepped back, but stopped when the floor creaked.

"Yes, yes," Elliana's mother said. "However, the promise you showed has not developed. It could be an advantage to have a great dancer in a family of our status, but it would be intolerable to have someone who is merely average."

"I shall be great."

"I should never have given in to your tricks and wheedling.

Unless you improve, Elliana, your father and I shall remove you from the school."

"You can't!"

"We can. Not only that, we'll put you where you won't be a nuisance to us any longer. Perhaps in the sanctuary—a temple dancer cloistered for life. Let the priestesses deal with you!" She sniffed. "Better yet, we shall betroth you to Lord Mardlehop."

"That old fatty!"

"Elliana Nautilus! That old fatty is one of the richest men in the kingdom. He is also one of the few men who will still have you now that word of your escapades with the street dancers has leaked out."

"No. Please. I promise to work harder. Only don't take me from the school. I won't marry him. I'll run away. I'll—"

"Hush, here come your little friends. I must go now, or I'll be late for my appointment. You heed my words, Elliana."

To Cerinthe's relief, she heard Elliana's mother walk back down the hall, where she greeted Elliana's friends and then left.

"We've been looking all over for you, Elliana," said a girl's voice a moment later. As the sound of their footsteps came down the hall, Cerinthe backed up again. Three girls turned the corner and saw her.

"You there!" Elliana, a tall girl with long, curly red hair, stood looking down her nose at Cerinthe. "What are you doing?"

"I was only," Cerinthe stammered, "only looking at the paintings."

Elliana stepped forward, her back straight and her chin

tucked, as though she balanced a half-full jug of water on her head.

"How long have you been here?" she asked, her green eyes still bright and furious.

"Only a moment." Embarrassed, Cerinthe looked away.

"You were snooping," Elliana said. "A snoop and a sneak, that's what you are."

The other girls tittered. All three wore royal blue dresses with pearly under-sleeves and underskirts. Pearl-studded combs held back their hair. They were perhaps a year older than Cerinthe.

"Look how the creature stares," said a girl with a face the color of chestnuts.

"Of course, Jasel," said Elliana. "She's a commoner. What else could you expect?"

Cerinthe frowned.

"Did you break anything?" Elliana asked. "Or touch anything? I hope you didn't foul this sculpture." She pointed to Kasakol's bent marble knee.

"Perhaps we should search beneath her cloak," said the third girl, who had dimpled cheeks. "She has most certainly stolen something."

"I haven't!" Cerinthe exclaimed.

"Away with you now, away!" Elliana's white hand shooed. Her fingernails were painted the same pale, glossy pink as a tellin shell. "You look like a servant—their hall is below stairs. Although I rather doubt they'll employ you." She flared her nostrils delicately and stared at the blackest tar stain on Cerinthe's skirt.

"I'm here for the Trial," Cerinthe said angrily, knowing she now smelled of sweat as well as fish. There had been no place to wash in the dressing room.

"Never!" Elliana exclaimed. "You? A dancer! With such hands and feet? Preposterous! Why my brother, Mareck, has smaller hands than you, and he's over six feet tall."

The girls giggled.

Cerinthe clenched her hands; they were big.

"Besides," said the dimpled girl, "you're far too stocky to be a dancer."

"And your hair," said Jasel, "why it's such a drab sort of ugly yellow-brown. You'll have simply no stage presence at all, I'm afraid, darling, as Daina Odonna would say."

They giggled again.

Cerinthe opened her mouth, clamped it shut, and then walked away down the hall.

"Where do you think you're going?" Elliana called. "You cannot simply wander about wherever you wish."

Cerinthe turned. "I'm going to the Kestrel Room, not that it's any of your concern. Daine Ambrose told us to wait there for the final list."

Elliana smiled. With her green eyes and red hair, she looked like a sea sprite. "I wouldn't bother."

"Why not?"

"Because you've been eliminated. Only those who have progressed to stage three will be on the final list."

Cerinthe crossed her arms. "Then why did Daine Ambrose tell us to wait?"

"So there will be an audience to applaud the winners, of

course," Elliana said, smoothing her blue broadcloth skirt. "I assure you, it was delightful—the cheers, the adulation. We remember, don't we, girls?"

They nodded.

Cerinthe stood speechless, feeling the rock in her stomach dragging her down again. Her momentary flicker of hope vanished.

"I'm terribly sorry," Elliana said sweetly, "but I'm afraid you simply were not good enough. You see, we take only the gifted. However, you might secure employment scrubbing our floors or cleaning our..." she cleared her throat "...slop pots." Her smile faded. The color of her eyes shifted from sea green to a sea blue flecked with white—a trait said to be a sign of the Sea Maid's favor. "Now, I'm telling you again," she said, her voice hard. "No one wants you. You are not good enough."

"Stoven and sunk!" Cerinthe cursed. "You are the meanest, rudest girl I've ever met!" And she fled down the hall.

Later that night, in a strange bed at the Seahorse Inn, Cerinthe wept beneath the quilt. She had been crying on and off ever since she had found her father in the Kestrel Room; they had left the school immediately. Cerinthe pressed the pillow against her mouth. How could she give up her dream of dancing? And worse, how could she go back to Normost? Her thoughts rolled like flotsam in the waves until at last, exhausted, she fell asleep.

The next afternoon, her eyes still felt scratchy and tired as she walked with Thordon along Harbor Road, the busy road that edged Majesty Bay.

"Those old daines and dainas must have sand in their eyes," Thordon said, yanking his brown woolen cap down on his head. "Kloud's Thunder! I watched you practice, and I think you're a fine dancer." He paused. "I bet your father was mad."

"No. He was relieved," Cerinthe said. She watched a ship, a two-masted pinnace, sailing out of the harbor, sailing away from Faranor. "I'm awfully glad the shipwrights took you," she managed to say.

Thordon shrugged, but his cheeks glowed. "Oh, that had nothing to do with me. Master Andal grew up with my father." He leaned against the top of the seawall; ten feet below, the water slapped the stony base. "At last," he said, looking out at the bay. "A place with enough ships!"

Cerinthe looked out too. Majesty Bay bustled with hundreds of ships; big ships and small, frigates and barques and coracles, ships being rowed out of harbor, and ships unfurling sails for voyages to every imaginable island in the kingdom. She counted fifteen schooners anchored beyond the breakwater. On twelve gigantic piers, longshoremen loaded and unloaded vast quantities of cargo.

"Normost has only one pier," she said, "and one quay." A southern wind blew off the harbor, a mild wind, very different from the fierce northwestern winds on Normost. It smelled of oak and spice.

"What happens next?" Thordon asked.

"We sail back tomorrow, on the evening tide." In the blue sky above, the gulls whimpered and shrieked. Cerinthe looked at the gleaming towers of Faranor, then at Thordon's face with its shadow of down above his lip. How could she leave?

"I want you to stay," Thordon said.

Cerinthe smiled.

"I talked to Master Andal," he added. "Tell your father to get a job in the shipyards. They need sailmakers."

"Tell him?" she said slowly. "You don't know my father. He'd never work in another man's workshop—and he hates Faranor."

"Convince him, then. He would do it for you."

"I can't ask him that."

Thordon frowned, which made his jaw square. "All right. Since you're too scared, I'll ask him."

"No!" she said, astounded.

"Then I think you should get a job. I'll find you one—cleaning fish or weaving nets."

"But dancing lessons cost a lot. A job like that would barely pay enough for me to live, let alone have lessons."

Thordon dug his boot between two stones and crushed a wild daisy.

"You aren't trying very hard to stay," he said.

Cerinthe hunched her shoulders. The water seemed to slap harder against the seawall. A sailor walked by, chatting to a pregnant woman beside him, who nodded and nodded, saying nothing.

"I didn't mean to…" Thordon said. "I just hoped you'd be in Faranor too. Hoped maybe we could see each other sometimes."

"That's all right." Cerinthe tried to smile. "I know what you meant."

They were silent.

"I've got to get back for the evening shift," Thordon said at last. "I expect you to write a lot of letters. Send them in care of Master Andal."

"I will. Fair winds be yours."

"And yours." Thordon took his hands out of his pockets,

looked at her, and shoved them back in. Then he walked away and disappeared into the crowd.

Cerinthe thought of returning to the inn but remembered that her father would still be out buying new tools and sailcloth. Besides, if she went there, she'd probably begin crying again, and what use was that? Instead, she walked on down Harbor Road, more determined than ever to find a way to stay in Faranor and become a dancer.

After three more blocks, she came to the market district, where booths and entertainers lined the landward side of the road. Vendors hawked everything from squawking chickens to the sextants used for navigation. The richer merchants, who carried goods imported from all over the kingdom, had shops with enormous glass windows.

Cerinthe watched a juggler tossing balls into the air and a mime imitating the people who passed. Children scampered everywhere, thin, ragged children who looked as though no one cared for them. On every corner musicians played lutes or harps or two-tiered bittie-bom drums. Cerinthe lingered near a group of roving dancers, wondering if she too might earn her bread by dancing for coins tossed into a bowl. At least then she could stay in Faranor and dance. But the women whirled like untrained children, and their costumes, cut low in the bodice and short in the skirt, made her blush.

Cerinthe turned away and bumped into a man in a green-striped smock who carried a bundle of pinwheels, each spinning at the end of a long stick.

"Buy or make way!" the man warned.

"Your pardon," Cerinthe called, dazzled by the twirling

gold and silver. She decided to spend one of the five shellnars her father had given her and ran after the man.

Her fingers had just brushed his sleeve when she heard someone singing. She stopped. The woman's voice was so deep and rich, so dark and bright, that for a moment Cerinthe thought she was hearing the Sea Maid. Though she looked, she couldn't find the streetsinger in the crowd, but the old, old song about the birth of Windward came through cloak and skin and bone, reaching for her heart.

> *In the beginning, was the Sea.*
> *Mother of all, the Goddess Nemaree.*
> *She crooned one note, an endless roaring.*
> *The roaring created wind,*
> *And the wind created light.*
>
> *Where the light shone through the sea,*
> *It made a wondrous new song.*
> *Each song rose through the mighty waters*
> *And became an island.*
> *Thus the archipelago was born.*
>
> *Nemaree married Kloud, God of the sky,*
> *And from their love the Sea Maid*
> *Was born upon the seafoam.*
> *She sings and sails in Her scallop shell*
> *Out where the sea meets the sky.*

She calls sailors home from the sea,
And calls hearts to their truth.
She calls the dying to the Black Ship
With its black sails unfurled....

Cerinthe clapped both hands over her ears. She turned and ran after the pinwheel vendor, who had almost disappeared. One of the pinwheels glinted a block away. She pushed through the crowd, darting this way and that, but the crowd was too thick. After a few blocks, she gave up.

Blinking back tears, trying to force the song from her mind, Cerinthe slumped against the seawall. The horizon stretched out endlessly, just as her life seemed to stretch bleakly before her. Oh why hadn't the royal school taken her? She wanted to run across the city, beat on those double doors, and scream at the doorman to let her in.

She looked around. She had reached the other edge of the market district, the far southern curve of the harbor where the gilded pleasure ships of the aristocracy were moored. Behind them, a steep hill towered above the city, jutting forward like an enormous figurehead overlooking the bay. To her right, an old man in a long brown robe was watching her. He sat on a stool with his feet together and his knees apart, which made his lower legs look like a pair of cloth-draped wings. Boldly, she stared back; there was something about him she liked. One wrinkled brown hand held a piece of wood, the other, a small knife.

"Afternoon, Sad Eyes," he said gravely.

"Hello." Cerinthe stepped closer and looked down at the carvings on the frayed blue carpet beside his feet. There were dolphins twisting, some wearing crowns; birds and butterflies with fantastic sweeping wings; lighthouses perched on cliffs; and a dozen different ships with their oak sails billowing in invisible winds.

"You'll find as many and more in my willow basket here," the man said. "See, if I put the cats out beside the birds they brawl worse than sailors come ashore."

Cerinthe glanced at him. His hawk-eyes flashed, though his mouth didn't smile. His face was as rough and brown as a toasted walnut. A length of red wool swathed over his head and draped around his shoulders.

"But it's not cats or dolphins you're wanting," he said, "is it, little Sad Eyes?"

"No. What I want couldn't possibly be in your basket," Cerinthe said.

"Hey, what's this?" He straightened. "Don't be so sure. Tell Old Skolla what you want, and maybe it's hidden in my basket."

Cerinthe sighed. "I want to study at the School of the Royal Dancers, but they don't want me."

"Ah-ho. Then little daina you are, not little Sad Eyes."

"I wasn't good enough," she said. "But there were only ten places. I've always dreamed of studying there."

"You're from the Northern Reach."

"How did you know?"

He chuckled. "I've sailed in all the reaches in the kingdom, little daina. I know a northern accent when I hear one. From which of the Misty Isles do you hail?"

"Normost. I don't want to go back, but I guess there's nothing else to do." She pictured Gwimma waiting on the pier,

Gwimma who always smelled of chamomile from the dispensary. Cerinthe shivered. She wouldn't be a healer ever again—no matter how much Gwimma scolded her.

"Normost, is it?" Old Skolla shaved off a twist of wood. "Then you're used to the powerful northwest winds that batter the isles up there, are you not?"

"I am."

He leaned toward her. His eyes were black with a sparkle of light, like whitecaps beneath a midnight moon. "And do you hide beneath your pillow when the storms come?"

"No! I love storms."

He smiled and leaned back. "Once Old Skolla sailed for seventeen days in the teeth of the northwest wind, trying to reach Borden Isle. But the storm blew and blew, relentless as an old granny stirring her soup." His hand went round. "So I took another tack. I snuggled up, sheltering in the lee of island after island for eight nights."

"What happened?"

"I reached my port. Sometimes, you have to creep sideways to get where you want to go. You can't point your sail too close to the wind or it will luff, and you'll stall, little daina, you'll stall for sure. You must catch just the right angle to go forward."

Although his words intrigued her, Cerinthe didn't know what to make of them. She lingered for a few more minutes, then said goodbye and started back toward the inn. Wrapped in gloomy thoughts, she took a wrong turn, ending up on a street that approached the Seahorse Inn from behind.

Hinges squeaked. Two women stepped out of the inn's back door. One woman held a broom.

"Mind you be scenting those sheets with lavender now, Mara," she said.

The other woman laughed. She wore an orange kerchief and carried a basket of soiled laundry on her hip.

"Are you having the queen herself board with you tomorrow then, Tessa? Is she coming down from the palace to sleep with the herring and oysters? Think maybe she'll take you into service?"

"What me?" exclaimed Tessa. "A servant to Her Majesty? Go on!" They laughed, and the washerwoman started down the street while Tessa swept the stoop.

As the broom swished, Cerinthe stood thinking. With over two hundred students at the royal school, not to mention teachers and staff, an army of servants would be needed. That was the answer! She would become a servant at the school and find a way to learn about dancing.

Then she sighed. Her father would never permit it. And could she bear being a maid where she had hoped to be a student?

"You're not trying very hard to stay," Thordon had said.

Above the inn, the towers of the city flamed gold and pink as the sun began to set. A thousand windows caught the light and glittered like diamonds. At that moment, Cerinthe knew she could bear anything, do anything, if only she could stay in Faranor and be a dancer.

The next morning, Cerinthe raised her hand to knock on the back door of the royal school, but at the last moment her knuckles came to rest soundlessly against the stout oak. Had it really been only two days ago that she had stepped through this very door for the Trial? This time, praise the Sea Maid, she was wearing clean, freshly ironed clothes and did not reek of fish. And this time she was alone. She had left her father a note saying she had found a job and would not return to Normost.

She took a deep breath, then reached over and swung the clapper on the brass bell, once, twice, three times. There. Now she couldn't back out. Her mouth tasted like acid. What if someone as rude as the front doorman were on duty here?

The latch lifted. A girl in a black uniform with a white apron, a girl little older than Cerinthe, opened the door.

"Yes?" she asked.

"May I speak to the housekeeper please? I've come to apply for service."

The girl's eyes skipped over Cerinthe. "Well, they do need someone for the laundry," she said. "It's terrible hard work though. I wouldn't want to do it." Her face was thin. Three brown curls poked out from her starched white cap.

"Hard work hasn't killed me yet," Cerinthe said.

The girl smiled and her thin face changed completely; she looked as gay as a sunbeam. "Then won't you please come in?"

Cerinthe crossed the threshold. At least she was inside the school again. It was a beginning.

"I'm Tayla," the girl said. "I'll take you to Mistress Blythe. She's the assistant to the head housekeeper and ever so much nicer. If she likes you, she'll put in a good word with Mistress Odue."

"Have you worked here long?" Cerinthe asked, following Tayla down the hall.

"Gosh yes," Tayla said. "Simply ages. I started in the scullery—lots of pots!—and worked my way up. It's not a bad place. The wages are fair; the food's plain but filling, and they don't overwork us young ones neither. The queen wouldn't hear of it," Tayla added grandly. "This is a royal institution, you know."

Cerinthe smiled. She hoped all the servants were this friendly. "Do you miss your family?"

"Not a bit," Tayla said. "Haven't got any to miss."

They turned down a second hall and approached the same back stairs that Cerinthe had taken on the day of the Trial.

Instead of going up to the second floor, as she had then, they went down one flight to the basement. Though plain, the basement smelled clean, and the whitewash on the walls looked fresh.

Somewhere in the seven floors above, girls were studying to be dancers. Cerinthe longed to be with them.

"Do you ever see any of the little dainas?" she asked Tayla.

"Oh yes. I do up the rooms of the pearls," Tayla said proudly.

"The pearls?"

"The little dainas' classes are named after precious jewels." Tayla held up her fingers. "The very littlest ones, nine to thirteen, they're the aggies—agates really, but everyone calls them aggies. Then the pearls, they're fourteen or so. Next come the emeralds, or ems. Then the rubies. And last, the very oldest girls about to go into the royal company," her voice grew reverent, "they're the diamonds."

Tayla stopped. "This is the servants' hall." She pushed open a swinging door and looked inside. "Mistress Blythe?"

"Yes, Tayla?"

"There's a girl here, quite a nice girl, wanting work. I remembered that somebody was wanted for the laundry."

"Show her in please, dear."

Tayla whispered to Cerinthe, "Fair winds be yours!"

"Thank you," Cerinthe whispered back and went in.

Mismatched, worn, but comfortable-looking furniture crowded the room: low, lacquered tables with chipped corners; four sofas—plaid, flowered, striped, and solid; two willow rockers; and a lamp with a cracked dome. Stuffing oozed through a patch on a red velvet chair. Mistress Blythe sat at a round oak table near the hearth, holding a piece of linen in her hands.

"They forgot the starch again," she said. "I don't know how many times I've told them." Her blue dress, which stretched over her plump body like the skin on a ripe plum, had a floppy white collar edged with lace. A little boy with wet cheeks sat beside her.

"It hurts!" he exclaimed and held up a cloth-wrapped finger. "I burnt it," he said to Cerinthe.

"Poor Dobbie," Mistress Blythe said. "How many times has Cook warned you to stay away from the stove? But, there, it will be better soon if you keep that cloth around it." She turned to Cerinthe. "What is your name, my dear?"

"I'm...Celinda." She had decided to change her name; Cerinthe was unusual, and someone might remember it from the Trial.

"You're not from Faranor, are you?"

"No. I just sailed in from the Northern Reach."

"Goodness," Mistress Blythe said, startled. "Aren't you a bit young to journey so far alone?"

"I'm thirteen," Cerinthe said, avoiding part of the question.

"Can't I take it off now?" Dobbie cried, wiggling on his chair. "Can't I? It's hurting me."

"No," Mistress Blythe said. "You need to soak your finger in bacon fat for at least an hour. That's a very bad burn."

Cerinthe winced. Gwimma had taught her that bacon fat was a terrible remedy for burns; it often made the wound putrefy. She opened her mouth to say, "Soak his finger in cold water, then treat it with an infusion of comfrey applied on a compress," but she clamped her jaw shut.

Mistress Blythe turned back to Cerinthe. "Have you any references, Celinda?"

"References?" She hadn't thought of that. "No, I don't."

"Have you been in service before?"

"No, but I learn quickly. I work hard, and I'm quite strong."

Mistress Blythe smiled. "Well, what do you know?"

"You mean about starching linens and that kind of thing?"

"Just tell me what you know, Celinda."

Dobbie sniffed.

Cerinthe looked at his finger again. How could she let him sit there with the wrong, and possibly harmful, remedy? But what did she really know about healing anyway? She wasn't certain of anything anymore, not after…besides, she had given it up.

Mistress Blythe cleared her throat.

"I know about herbs," Cerinthe began. "I know how to find and grow them, when to harvest them, and how to use them in—cooking. I can sew a good, straight seam. And I can read and write too."

Mistress Blythe folded the linen tablecloth into thirds and said nothing.

"I can make jam and jelly," Cerinthe rushed on, desperate to convince her. "And I know how to varnish wood." The laundry; they needed someone for the laundry. "I know how to catch rainwater in a barrel and wash the sheets in it. I dry them in the sun, iron them smooth, and make up a bed so it smells fresh and sweet. So it's nice to sleep in."

Cerinthe thought of her own bed, of home, and Normost. "I know about tides," she said. "I can row five miles before my arms start to ache. I know where the crabs hide in the rocks and how to dig clams from the sand. And I know the sound of the Sea Maid's voice on water or wind."

Mistress Blythe stopped folding, and the tablecloth swung from her fingers. Her watery blue eyes stared at Cerinthe. They looked as weary as her father's often did after he had stitched sails all day.

"I know how to brew a cup of soothing sagan tea," Cerinthe added. "It soothes tired eyes. I mix it with honey and lemon and…" Cerinthe stopped. She felt suddenly guilty, thinking of how frantic and furious her father would be when he found her note.

"You sound like a very knowledgeable girl, Celinda," Mistress Blythe said, smiling. She looked less tired. "Very well. I shall take you to Mistress Odue. The final decision is hers."

After coaxing Dobbie into the kitchen with a plate of cookies, Mistress Blythe led Cerinthe up to the main floor. Her boots sank into the thick royal blue rug. She waited in the hall outside Mistress Odue's room while Mistress Blythe spoke with her.

"No references!" a sharp voice exclaimed. "The Northern Reach and shabby clothes? She could be anything!"

"As though I'm a toad or a murderer," Cerinthe mumbled, uncertain whether to laugh or scream. What would Thordon say if he could see her now? She shook her head. A common girl from the Northern Reach was barely worthy to be a servant here, let alone a student. How could she ever have dreamed otherwise? That horrible Elliana girl had been right.

The door opened.

"Come in, dear," Mistress Blythe said. "Mistress Odue will see you now."

Inside the room, oak chests and cabinets with brass locks crowded the walls. Mistress Odue stooped over a huge square desk and pushed up the tiny gold-rimmed glasses pinching her nose. Her collar bristled into two crisp points. Her chin looked as sharp as an arrow, pointing to the square black buttons that marched in a line down her white blouse. When she eyed Cerinthe, one corner of her mouth twisted.

"You are Celinda?" she asked. She spoke as if she had a mouth full of coins.

"I am."

"You will answer thus: Yes, mistress."

"Yes, mistress."

"Mistress Blythe has recommended you for a position in the laundry, even though you have no references." Mistress Odue pursed her lips. "We will take you on trial for one month. During that time you will learn your duties on half wages. Stealing, lying, clumsiness, or laziness will result in instant dismissal. Rank among the servants must be strictly followed. I stand for no nonsense, Celinda."

"Yes, mistress," Cerinthe said.

"You will be working under the direct supervision of Mistress Dalyrimple, head of the laundry. But, as this is Her Majesty's school, you are ultimately working for the queen. Remember that. Behave accordingly."

"Yes, mistress," Cerinthe said. She hoped this trial would turn out better than the last.

Mistress Odue tapped her fingertip on her desk. "You may go."

Cerinthe walked out of the housekeeper's room to begin her

new life in the School of the Royal Dancers, not, as she had always dreamed, as a little daina, but as a laundry maid.

Chapter Six

Scrub harder, Celinda!"
Mistress Dalyrimple scolded, bending over the washtub. She
tucked the hem of her pumpkin-colored skirt beneath her belt
to keep it out of the water streaming across the stone floor. Her
double chins, which were shiny and moist from the steam in
the air, wobbled as she talked.

"Sluggard! Dreamer! Get that petticoat spotless! Don't know
where you've worked before, but we've got standards here."

"Yes, mistress," Cerinthe said and scraped her knuckles
against one of the washboard rungs. She flinched. After
working for five days in the laundry, her hands were chapped.
She didn't mind that—at home her hands had often been
chapped from seawater and chores—but here the harsh, yellow
laundry soap made her skin crack and bleed.

"And make haste, girl," Mistress Dalyrimple added. "That

stack of petticoats beside you is taller than Chesler Tower!"

"Yes, mistress."

With a disgusted snort, Mistress Dalyrimple waddled to the next of the fifteen tubs.

"How do you like life in the damp dungeon?" whispered Marese, a peaked, ten-year-old girl scrubbing beside Cerinthe. Marese sniffed, then wiped her nose on her grey sleeve. All of the laundry maids had colds.

"It's…fine," Cerinthe said. "Just fine." She lifted her bare foot out of the water and, standing like a heron on one leg, glumly considered her new life.

From six in the morning until six in the evening, she washed clothes in the basement. At night, she slept in a windowless room with twenty other girls. She hadn't seen the sky in days. Although the laundry had slits of windows near the ceiling, the steam and damp never seemed to go out, and the light never seemed to come in. On Normost she had done the washing outside where she could hear the waves, watch the fishing boats, and smell the scent of herbs blowing from Gwimma's garden.

Cerinthe sighed. When she turned the petticoat inside out, she noticed the name stitched on the waistband: Elliana of Nautilus.

Stoven and sunk! Cerinthe slapped the petticoat against the washboard. Considering all the clothes she washed, this was bound to have happened sooner or later. She would have preferred later though—or never. Her brush rubbed faster and faster until the soapsuds flew.

She had only herself to blame for her predicament. She was like a spiny old crab that had crawled into a pot after bait. And now she was stuck! Cerinthe leaned down to rinse the petticoat, and her back began to ache. How could she ever have imagined she would learn about dancing by being a servant? Dirty clothes were all that she had seen of the dancers so far, and she wasn't likely to see anything more. Laundry maids were never allowed above stairs.

Cerinthe twisted the water out of the petticoat. What are you made of anyway, Cerinthe Gale? she asked herself. You said you could bear anything to stay in Faranor and become a dancer. Does someone who can row five miles against the tide give up so easily? She sloshed through the water, dunked Elliana's petticoat in the final rinse tub, and fed it through the wringer. She felt a surge of wicked delight when the petticoat emerged from the rollers as flat as a paper doll.

A bell clanged.

"One o'clock at last," Marese said. "I thought it wasn't never coming. I do hope there's bread pudding."

The servants stopped work and ate bean soup, clamcakes, and rolls with butter and marmalade in the servants' dining hall. Tayla waved to Cerinthe from the under housemaids' table across the room.

"Someday I'll get promoted and wear a uniform just like Tayla's," said Marese, sitting beside Cerinthe. "All black and white and crisp." The laundry and scullery maids wore limp, grey dresses, aprons, and caps, which prompted the higher-ranking servants to call them "smudges." Even Cerinthe's nightgown was grey, she noticed, when she pulled it on late that night.

For hours she lay awake in her bunk. In the black stillness

her courage at last deserted her, and she cried beneath the covers. She longed for the sea, for the music of the tide that had lulled her to sleep since cradle days.

She thought of Thordon, alone too in this enormous city, and of her father sailing alone back to Normost. She imagined how Normost looked at night from her bedroom window: the herb garden a blur of humps and spikes; the beach a slick of black; and the rocks beyond rising like black dreams from the surf. The lighthouse on Dolmar Bluff would flash and all would be bright. After eight heartbeats of darkness, the light always shone again. But, as she imagined it all, the light did not shine, though she counted past eight to nine, to ten and eleven, and she screamed as the rocks reared toward her....

Cerinthe sat straight up. Around her, the other girls breathed softly in their bunks. It was only a nightmare—she'd had many since her mother had died. She lay down again, squashed her pillow against her face, and prayed to the Sea Maid. *Sing to me, please. I long for Your voice. Take away the nightmares. Bring me light and strength.* Long minutes passed, and though Cerinthe waited and waited, no voice sang.

The next day crept by as drearily as all the others. Cerinthe finished her pile of petticoats and went doggedly into the next room for more. There, towering over mountains of dirty laundry, Mistress Dalyrimple stood sorting clothes. Her arms whirled. She tossed the clothes through the air so fast that a breeze blew through the room.

"What do you mean she wants them now?" she hollered at an under housemaid who hovered in the doorway. "Astonishment! Outrage! No one told me!" The under housemaid merely shrugged and left.

Mistress Dalyrimple stopped whirling her arms and clapped both hands on her hips. "What am I expected to do, practice mind-reading magic?" She spotted Cerinthe. "You!"

"Yes, mistress?"

"If Nordine's finished ironing those bandages, get them to Mistress Blythe. They're wanted in the dispensary on the third floor. Haste!"

Cerinthe ran to the ironing room, found the bandages, and then put on her shoes and stockings. She went to the servants' hall, but Mistress Blythe was neither there nor in the kitchen. Who would see to the bandages?

"Pardon me—" Cerinthe tried to speak to one person after another, but no one would listen. Finally, exasperated, she blocked the path of the next servant who came down the hall. Unfortunately, the woman was an upper housemaid. She wore a black taffeta dress, which she twitched back and forth, and a white linen apron trimmed with lace.

"—and the bandages are needed right away," Cerinthe finished explaining. "So could you please take them up to the dispensary? You know I'm not allowed above stairs."

The woman arched her eyebrows, plucked so fine they looked like frowns embroidered on her forehead. "I am engaged in the important task of preparing a tea tray for Daina Odonna herself. And I don't run errands for smudges. Find an under housemaid." She flounced away.

"But what if somebody's hurt?..." Cerinthe called, but the woman did not look back.

"Old scum-guts," Cerinthe said. Now what? If only she could find Tayla, but Tayla would be upstairs cleaning the pearls' rooms. Cerinthe walked to the back stairs at the end of the hall and looked up. Why not take the bandages herself? She put her foot on the first step, then hesitated. If anyone saw her, she might be dismissed.

Someone might be hurt, though, just as she had told the maid. Someone might be lying in pain, be bleeding or bruised. Cerinthe shuddered. Her head drooped and her chin rested on top of the stack of bandages.

Wait. Going to the dispensary did not mean she was a healer. Delivering bandages was a maid's task, and she was a maid.

Before she could change her mind, Cerinthe raced up the stairs. She passed the first floor, the second floor, and stopped at the third, where music flittered through the air. Her eyes began to sparkle. Perhaps this was her first chance to see a dancing class! She hurried down the hall, looking at every door she passed, but every door was shut.

Then three students in royal blue dresses approached from the opposite end of the hall. Cerinthe flattened herself against the wainscoting—she was caught above stairs! But the girls merely glanced at her and looked away as if she were nothing but a piece of furniture. Relieved, Cerinthe turned into the right wing.

A door on her left stood open. A dancing class? She crept up and peered inside. Instead of dancers, she saw shelves filled with blue-and-white porcelain jars. Below them, on a long mahogany counter, was a brass scale for measuring medicine.

Cerinthe sighed. It was only the dispensary.

"Hello?" she called from the threshold.

No one answered. Six closed doors—leading to individual sick rooms, she guessed—stood along the far wall.

"I brought the bandages," she called louder. The silence buzzed in her ears. She had never dreamed that she'd find no one there, that she might have to go in herself. She had not set foot inside a dispensary since the day her mother had died.

"I'm here as a smudge," she whispered fiercely, "that's all." She walked straight to the center of the room, where sunlight poured through the tall, sweeping windows. One window was open in spite of the cool, autumn day, and the white curtains billowed like sails against the blue sky. She saw no sign of any crisis.

She laid the bandages beside the scale and looked up at the exquisite jars. Each bore the name of an herb or medicinal plant, fired in scrolling blue letters on the white porcelain: arnica, bay, chamomile, comfrey, elmswood, halibane, lemon balm, and others she did not recognize.

Cerinthe reached for the chamomile, but her hand dropped to her side. Then her fingernails dug into her palm. What was she afraid of? It was only chamomile. She grabbed the jar and opened the lid, expecting the fragrance of apple, but the dried leaves smelled musty. The elmswood leaves were old too. She opened a crock marked "calendula cream," thinking it might soothe her chapped hands, only to find mold flourishing on the top. Cerinthe wrinkled her nose. For a "royal institution," as Tayla called the school, it didn't have much of a dispensary. The jars were beautiful, yes, but their contents!

Cerinthe thought of Gwimma's dispensary with the plain earthenware jars, with the sea air making even the bandages smell of salt. She constantly preserved fresh herbs and threw away the old ones when they lost their potency. Bundles of drying plants hung from the rafters. Cerinthe would grind them in the mortar and pestle and...

Suddenly she felt a cramp, then a sharp pain directly beneath her heart.

"Mama," she said, "oh Mama, I'm sorry." She sagged against the mahogany counter. No! Cerinthe slapped it with her palm and the scale rattled. She would not think about that terrible day; she would not. She should never have come to the dispensary.

As Cerinthe turned toward the door, she noticed a white bowl gleaming on a small table in the corner. It was shaped like a scallop shell, with delicate ribs and fluted edges. It pulled her like the moon does the tide. She lifted it up and walked toward the window.

Light splashed into the bowl. The warm pink of her palms showed through glass so thin it was nearly transparent. The Sea Maid Herself might have spun this bowl from light and wind and shell. Didn't the priestesses say that the Sea Maid skimmed over the waves in a scallop shell pulled by six blue seahorses?

Cerinthe looked in the luminous glass, and faces floated into her mind, the faces of people she had treated: Onnor, an old woman with painful joints; Spiri, a little boy with endless cuts and scrapes; Tod, the fisherman with his cough; and Dilla, bent with back pain. After her mother's death, Cerinthe had referred them all to Gwimma.

"What are you doing?" a voice asked.

Cerinthe jumped. The scallop bowl slipped from her hands, crashed to the floor, and shattered into hundreds of pieces.

Chapter Seven

"No!" Cerinthe cried, and knelt with her hands reaching out. "I've broken it." The sparkling fragments of the scallop bowl lay scattered across the dispensary floor. "And it was so…"

"Don't cut yourself," a voice warned.

"…so beautiful." Cerinthe dropped her empty hands into her lap. This loss woke her deeper one, and she felt half blinded by the stinging, too-familiar pain. At that moment, more than anything else under sea or sky, she wanted the luminous bowl in her hands again. But wanting would not make it so; her mother's death had taught her that.

Quiet footsteps crossed the room. Cerinthe blinked tears from her eyes and looked up.

A woman stood before the tall windows, the sky framing her with a brilliant, hazy blue. Her face had the tinge of golden-brown kelp. Her skin gleamed, set off by the white muslin robe that rippled in soft folds from her shoulders to her feet. A thick, brown braid fell to her waist. She was looking down at the pieces on the floor.

"I brought up some bandages," Cerinthe explained. "The under housemaid said it was urgent. I couldn't find anyone else, and I was afraid somebody might be hurt, and then I saw the bowl, and—"

The woman looked up at her.

Cerinthe realized she was only making excuses. "I'm terribly sorry," she said. "I shouldn't have touched it."

"Only Nemaree knows the answer to that," the woman said. "However, I startled you; it was my fault that you dropped the bowl. I apologize."

Surprised, Cerinthe sat back on her heels. Perhaps the bowl was not so valuable as she thought. The woman, who had two canvas sacks hanging over her arm, knelt carefully on the other side of the pieces. She picked up the largest one, the size of her blunt thumbnail.

"What—I mean, who are you?" Cerinthe asked.

"I am Mederi Grace."

"A mederi!" Cerinthe sprang to her feet. Healers with evil, magical powers acquired in mysterious schools were called "mederi." Legend said that they could heal, or kill, with a glance. Everyone on Normost feared them, although no one Cerinthe knew had ever seen a mederi. Gwimma had scorned the notion that healing could be learned from books and magic spells. An older folk healer had passed his knowledge along to her.

Mederi Grace put the piece in her lap. "I gather you've never met a mederi before?"

Cerinthe shook her head, backing away.

"I assure you, I don't bite." Mederi Grace held out her hands; the palms were rough with calluses. An intricate henna pattern of diamonds, swirls, and dots spiraled from her wrists to her forearms. "And I couldn't turn you into a sea urchin even if I wished," she added. "Which is good, because I would find that tempting at the moment." A sparkle spread from her eyes across her face, until her entire body seemed radiant with joy.

Cerinthe knelt again—but not too close.

"Good," the mederi said. "You have courage. I know what atrocious tales are told of us in the Reaches. What is your name?"

"I'm Cer…Celinda."

"Thank you for bringing up the bandages, Celinda."

"But no one's hurt. Or did you already cure her with…" Cerinthe lowered her voice, "…your powers?"

"Oh, yes. I waved one hand like this, blinked three times, and made her swallow ten roasted seagulls. It cured the broken arm, but now the patient has a dreadful stomachache." The mederi laughed a clear, ringing laugh.

Cautiously, Cerinthe smiled.

"I wish healing were as simple as that." Mederi Grace sighed. "Yes, fortunately no one is ill or injured. Mistress Blythe asked me to replenish the dispensary."

Cerinthe watched her slide the canvas sacks off her arm. Why did a mederi need a dispensary? Where was the magic in herbs and bandages? "The elmswood and chamomile are musty," she managed to say. "And there's mold on the calendula cream."

"I'm not surprised. The school hasn't had its own mederi since the outbreak of Yulion Plague in the south. There were few of us to begin with, and there's so much need all over the kingdom." She looked at the floor. "I want to collect all of these fragments. They may be too small to glue together, but sometimes the Master Potter can work miracles."

Cerinthe helped her gather them up. After they placed the bigger pieces in one of the sacks, Cerinthe found a broom and swept up even the tiniest shards. These, too, the mederi kept, wrapped in a bandage.

"In what part of the school do you work, Celinda?" she asked.

"Down in the dunge…I mean, the laundry." But not much longer, she realized, once Mistress Odue learned about the broken bowl. Cerinthe gripped the broom handle. It seemed that she had failed this trial too. Mistress Odue would be only too happy to dismiss her. She would be homeless and destitute in a city already crawling with beggar children.

Mederi Grace twined her fingers into her braid, her brown eyes softening as if she sensed Cerinthe's thoughts. Maybe she did; people said the mederi practiced mind magic.

"I'll pay for the bowl out of my wages," Cerinthe said, "as soon as I'm paid. I only started six days ago, and they don't pay me anything for a month."

"That's very gracious, but I'm afraid it would take more than you could earn in your lifetime."

"It would?"

"Yes. When the school was founded four hundred years ago, Queen Scallopia presented that bowl to the mederi who tended the dancers. It was priceless." The glass tinkled inside the sack as Mederi Grace placed it on the counter.

"Perhaps we should have kept it under lock and key," she added, "instead of using it for a water basin. But I believe that things should be used, even rare and valuable things, otherwise they lose their essential nature. That's far worse than being broken."

Cerinthe leaned the broom beside the table where the scallop bowl had stood. Its luminous shape still seemed to quiver in the air so that she could almost…almost touch it. If only she knew the right words, magic words, she could reshape the light and dust and shadow, and make the bowl appear. But she didn't know them. Her hand fell. No matter what she did, she could never replace the bowl. Cerinthe braced herself and turned, expecting the mederi's next words would be an order to summon Mistress Odue.

Mederi Grace opened the second sack. "Don't concern yourself about the bowl. It was an accident, so we will say nothing more about it." She took the jar of chamomile from the shelf.

"But what about Mistress Odue?"

"The bowl belonged to the mederi, not to her. Now, will you hold this sack for me?"

Cerinthe was so amazed and grateful that she couldn't speak, but simply took the sack and held it open while Mederi Grace poured in the chamomile. Mistress Dalyrimple would be raging over her absence, but Cerinthe didn't care. She felt awed, if still frightened, to be in a mederi's presence. Again and again her eyes were drawn to the mederi's face, that of a woman in midlife. It was a strong face; even the lines had vitality. At the same time, it had a serenity that seemed wrested from struggle—like the sea palms that grew on beaches pounded by the fiercest waves.

"I'm surprised that you're not a little daina," Mederi Grace said. "You certainly carry yourself like one. Dancing is an arduous calling; it can cause such serious injuries—of both body and soul."

Soul? Cerinthe wondered.

"The school simply must have a mederi in residence again, or at least a properly trained healer," Mederi Grace added, shaking out the old elmswood. "Mistress Blythe tries her best but she has too much to do and no training."

"I know," Cerinthe said, "she smears bacon fat on burns."

Mederi Grace frowned. "I'll have to speak to her about that. Do you know something about healing, Celinda? You certainly have a healer's hands. They're wonderfully strong and capable looking, though a bit chapped at the moment. We'll have to see what we can do about that." She opened another jar, and the bitter smell of glimroot flooded the room.

Cerinthe froze. Her eyes blurred. Her thoughts grew fuzzy, and for once she could not stop the memory that always rasped at the edge of her mind: the memory of the day she had found the strip of metal on the beach and the day that followed, the terrible day that her mother died.

Chapter Eight

On that day last winter, Cerinthe found the strip of metal lying on the seaweed necklace left by the high tide. In the early dawn, the sand rippled darkly down to the sea, and the sun seemed reluctant to rise through the black clouds to the east. She shivered. No wind blew, and the water was as smooth as the touch of her mother's hand on her cheek.

Cerinthe picked up the metal strip, avoiding the sharp, jagged edges. It was as long as her arm and as wide as the blade of an oar. Red and blue patterns etched by the sea salt shimmered across the surface. The sea had worked its usual magic, transforming a common, discarded thing into something wondrous. Cerinthe carried it up from the beach and leaned it against the well.

When her mother came to draw water for the breakfast

porridge, with her skirts tucked up to avoid the dew, she cut her leg on the metal. The gash stretched from her ankle to her knee. Although Cerinthe cleaned the cut well, the wound-fever came fast and hard. Gwimma was away on the far side of the island birthing a baby. Cerinthe applied poultice after poultice and tried every cure for infection that she knew, but, by late the next day, Eilisha Gale lay dying.

"She's getting better, isn't she?" Cerinthe's father asked, standing outside the dispensary doorway. "What's that stench? What are you doing now?"

Cerinthe, frantically grinding glimroot with mortar and pestle, tried to remember all that Gwimma had taught her. Used incorrectly, the glimroot could kill. Was it five pinches with six drops of oil of basomile, or six pinches with five drops of basomile?

"She's not better," Cerinthe said. "She's worse. I'm making an infusion of glimroot."

"Glimroot? But that's dangerous." He tugged on his beard.

"I don't know what else to do! After she drinks it, I'll lance her leg." The pestle trembled in Cerinthe's hand. "I have to drain the putrescence."

She finished grinding the root, measured six pinches into a bowl, and began adding the basomile, one drop, two drops, three. In spite of the open door and window, the room reeked from the putrefied wound, the fetid smell of something rotting in seawater.

"Are you sure—" her father began.

"I'm sure of nothing!" Cerinthe said. "Please. I ask you again. Row over and get the mederi who is visiting Thamas

Isle." She had been begging her father to go for hours.

"No," he said. "I'll fetch Gwimma."

Cerinthe slammed the bowl down on the table. She ran to the door and pulled her father back to the bedside.

"Look!" she said, peeling off the poultice. Her mother's leg was swollen from ankle to thigh, streaked with red, and it stank like a whale dead on the beach.

"In Nemaree's name." Her father covered his nose, his eyes bulging above his hand.

"Do you see now?" Cerinthe asked. "The corruption creeps higher and higher. She'll die…unless…I think her leg must come off."

"No!"

"I don't know how to do that. And neither does Gwimma, or she would have taught me. Only a mederi, I fear them too, but the stories say they have the magic to—"

"No!" he shouted again. "I won't have my wife butchered by some spell-weaver! Gwimma will know what to do. Eilisha won't die. You know nothing—you're only a child!" And he ran out of the dispensary. Cerinthe followed.

"The mederi!" she screamed after him. "Bring the mederi!" But he was already halfway to the dock.

"May we help, Cerinthe?" asked Magrit, one of the women who had hovered about the dispensary all day.

"Only if one of you will bring the mederi."

All of the women looked at the ground. When Eilisha Gale moaned from her bed, Magrit put her hand to her mouth but wouldn't meet Cerinthe's eyes.

"Stoven and sunk!" Cerinthe cried, thinking of the many

times she had helped them with an illness. "A shark's got more honor than the lot of you!" And she stepped inside and slammed the door. She squeezed the last drop of basomile into the glimroot. If only she hadn't brought the metal up from the beach. If only she hadn't left it by the well. If only, if only…

She picked up the kettle and poured hot water over the mixture. Her hands shook so much that half of the water splashed on the table.

"Cerinthe," her mother whispered.

"Mama?"

"Get the seagull."

Cerinthe ran to the house and returned with the crystal seagull that her mother had bought long ago on her one glorious trip to Faranor, the highlight of her life.

"It's yours now," Eilisha Gale said. "Be a dancer. A great artist." Her eyes closed. "Promise to go to the royal school. Go to Faranor."

"I promise. But you'll be fine."

"No. It's coming. I see—"

"I won't let you die!" Cerinthe cried. But she could not stop the swelling nor stem the creeping corruption. Only the glimroot might. Once it had steeped, she strained the liquid into a cup. Outside, the surf began to boom as the tide shifted from the quiet of high slack and began to go out. Cerinthe lifted her mother's head.

"Try to swallow, Mama," she urged. Eilisha Gale tried, and some of the infusion trickled down her throat. The horrible streaks on her leg stretched almost to her hip.

"I'm sorry," Cerinthe whispered. "This will hurt, but I must drain the putrescence." Her mother's head rolled sideways; she was unconscious again.

Cerinthe prepared the bandages. After wiping the knife with spirits, she turned it back and forth above the candle flame, where the heat was fierce but wouldn't foul the blade with soot. A golden ball of light shone on the metal. Cerinthe tried to study the bloated leg with detachment, to consider where to begin the incision, but her stomach pitched. She turned away. Her glance landed on the window, and out of habit she looked to the sea for strength. Instead of strength, what she saw filled her with horror.

Out upon the sea sailed a black ship with black sails unfurled, though the day was windless. It sped over the waves, spitting spray. Seven silver dolphins swam to port and seven more to starboard. Cerinthe knew what ship it was, even though she had only heard it described in tales. It was the ship that carried away the souls of the dead.

"No!" she shouted, closing her eyes, yet she could still see the Black Ship coming. She had to stop it but couldn't move.

Then, over the hiss of the tide going out, over the reedy dolphins' cries, a voice began to sing. Pure and clear, the voice of the Sea Maid soared up, reverberating like an ancient bell. She sang and she sang, a song with no words, an aria of light perceived by the heart. Cerinthe's hands steadied. She opened her eyes, lowered the knife, and swiftly, surely, cut a clean straight line.

But still the Black Ship came.

❀

"Celinda!" Mederi Grace grabbed Cerinthe's shoulders. "Celinda, what's wrong? Are you ill?"

"Mama!" Cerinthe cried. She blinked and suddenly found herself back in the royal school's dispensary, pulling at the collar on her grey uniform. She was drenched in sweat. "I can't breathe!" she cried.

She ran out of the room; away from the smell of the glimroot; away from the memory that her mother had died later that night. "It was the glimroot," Gwimma had raged in her grief, even though she had seen the extent of the infection. "You should never have used it!"

Cerinthe raced down the hall and up a flight of stairs. Footsteps came running after her. She veered down another hall and tried a door. It was locked. The footsteps came closer. Cerinthe ran around a corner and grasped a door latch. It lifted. She flung open the door, darted in, and slammed it behind her.

She leaned back, panting, and froze.

Along the barre attached to the wall, a group of older girls stopped dancing. They wore short royal blue tunics, pink hose, and pink dancing slippers. Two girls stood with their hands on the pianoforte, which they had been using for a barre. One girl, who was tall and radiant, had honey-gold hair. The other, still half turned away, had the melancholy eyes of a doe. All of the girls wore diamond-studded combs in their hair, and all of them were staring, astonished, at Cerinthe.

With a swirl of black skirts, a woman rose from her chair beside the mirrored wall. It was Daina Odonna. Cerinthe gasped. Then she saw her reflection in the mirror: a grey smudge who had lost her cap.

"You!" Daina Odonna said. "From the Trial! Why wasn't I informed?"

"Poor child," murmured the doe-eyed girl. "She's lost."

"And why are you wearing that horrible grey dress?" Daina Odonna asked, walking toward her.

"I'm sorry!" Cerinthe exclaimed. "I'm so sorry! I didn't mean to. I didn't know what else to do...." She wrenched open the door and ran down the hall.

"I order you to stop!" the daina called, but Cerinthe flew down the back stairs, one flight, then another and another.

"Smudge!" cried a startled upper housemaid dusting the banister. "Just what do you think you're doing up here?"

Cerinthe slipped past. She had to get out of the school. After one last flight, she burst out onto the main floor. She ran down the ornate hall—beneath tiered chandeliers, past tapestries, painted cherubs, and chairs upholstered in velvet too exquisite to ever dream of sitting on—toward the Grand Entry with its carved double doors. And there, examining a picture on a golden easel, stood Mistress Blythe, Mistress Odue, and a man. They heard Cerinthe's running footsteps and turned in alarm. The man's jaw dropped.

"Cerinthe!" he shouted.

"Father?" Cerinthe froze. "Father!" she cried again and flung herself into his arms.

"Cerinthe?" said Mistress Blythe, her hands fluttering at her collar. "Then what you suspected is true, sir. Celinda is Cerinthe!"

Cerinthe's father hugged her tightly. "I thought you were lost, kidnapped, or murdered in this cursed city!

What got into you, Daughter? Running away like that?"

"I'm so glad to see you," Cerinthe said, still breathless.

"We've been looking everywhere for you," Mistress Blythe said.

Cerinthe pressed her cheek into her father's wool vest. "There was no one else to take the bandages, and I thought someone might be hurt...."

"No child," Mistress Blythe said, "I meant—"

"This is most irregular!" Mistress Odue interrupted. The black buttons on her blouse were all askew. "Most irregular indeed!"

"Look, Cerinthe." Her father pointed to the picture on the easel, but it wasn't a picture, rather a parchment covered with ornate calligraphy. Cerinthe leaned closer and read:

Day of Trial / List of New Students
Accepted by The School of the Royal Dancers
In the Year Forty-Two of the Reign of
Her Majesty,
Queen Endorian Dorthea Mistral
Of the Royal House of Seaborne

Then Cerinthe read the first name on the list:

Cerinthe Gale of Normost

Chapter Nine

Four hours later, after a long, luxurious bath in Mistress Blythe's private rooms, Cerinthe dried her hair on a towel. Her smudge's uniform had disappeared, and she slipped into the fluffy blue robe that had been left in its place. She traced the words embroidered on the left shoulder beneath the queen's crest: The School of the Royal Dancers.

It seemed impossible that she had been first, first on the list! First all along! She could hardly believe it yet; so much had happened so quickly. Cerinthe gave her head a final brisk rub with the towel, thinking it might wake her from this incredible dream. It didn't.

"Cerinthe Gale," she said to her reflection in the mirror, "you are a student, a little daina. Otherwise you'd be washing this robe, not wearing it." As soon as she found pen and paper, she would send word to Thordon.

After combing her hair, Cerinthe walked into a tiny sitting room, where a fire snapped on the hearth. She curled up in one of the overstuffed green chairs and touched the lace doily on the armrest. The chapped skin on her fingers looked odd against the lace. She turned her sore hands back and forth; they didn't look like hands that should be coming out of the sleeves of an elegant blue robe.

Mistress Blythe opened the door. "Here's a cup of sagan mint tea, my dear. I thought it might calm you down after all the excitement."

"Thank you." Cerinthe took the china cup, delicately painted with pink rosebuds, and sipped the tea.

"I hope I made it as well as you do," Mistress Blythe said. "Remember our first conversation? Your brewing description was perfectly delicious. I think it made me decide to recommend you to Mistress Odue." She laughed.

"I'm glad you did."

"To think you were working right under our noses while we were scouring the city for you." Mistress Blythe settled down in the other chair and smoothed her collar. "Daina Odonna said you were one of the most promising applicants she had ever seen. My, she was furious when you vanished! And fancy your hoping to get into the school by becoming a maid. You're certainly a most determined and resourceful girl. Your father said so too."

Cerinthe lowered her cup and stared at the steam curling out like misty sails.

"Hard saying good-bye to him, was it?" Mistress Blythe asked gently.

"Awful," Cerinthe whispered. Her father would sail from Faranor at dawn, but no one could take her to see him leave. "Can't I go to the harbor alone?" she asked. "I promise to come straight back."

"I am sorry, but the city's full of strangers. We can't risk letting students go beyond the courtyard. It's one of our strictest rules."

Cerinthe's throat swelled as though she had swallowed a raw oyster that wouldn't slide down. She should be happy; the Sea Maid had answered her prayers at last. Beyond all likelihood, she was a little daina at the royal school.

Her pale blue eyes warm, Mistress Blythe leaned forward and patted Cerinthe's knee.

"You will begin classes the day after tomorrow," she said. "Mederi Grace has recommended a day of rest for you first. And I quite agree. Especially since Daina Odonna says you will be placed with the pearls instead of the agates."

"The pearls? But I'm too young."

"You will be the only thirteen-year-old, that's true, but the daina believes you are too advanced for the aggies."

Cerinthe set her cup on the side table. Elliana and her friends were pearls. Elliana! It was she who had led Cerinthe to believe she had no chance. "...you've been eliminated. Only those who have progressed to stage three will be on the final list...."

"Mistress Blythe," Cerinthe asked slowly, "why wasn't my name called with the others at the end of the second stage of the Trial?"

"It certainly would have saved a great deal of trouble. You see, Daina Odonna knew she wanted you, but she still had to decide among the others. She assumed, incorrectly as it turned out, that you would wait in the Kestrel Room for the final list."

A log collapsed in the fireplace, and Cerinthe watched the orange embers pulse. Elliana had known there was a chance. How could anyone be so mean?

"Believe me, the daina has changed the procedure." Mistress Blythe stood. "I'll send up a pearl's uniform, and we'll get you all settled in your new room. The housemother who usually sees to that is away." She turned to go, then stopped.

"Oh, I nearly forgot." Mistress Blythe pulled a little round tin from her pocket. "Mederi Grace made a salve for your hands." She gave it to Cerinthe and left.

Pleased but wary of mederi's magic, Cerinthe looked down at the tin. A few minutes after she had found her father beside the easel, the mederi had found her and questioned her closely about her trance in the dispensary. "I'm fine," Cerinthe had insisted, evading the questions.

Now, she sank back in the chair cushions and thought of the glimroot and her mother. It had been horrible, remembering it all so clearly.

Oh Sea Maid, Cerinthe prayed. *Tell Mama I'm a little daina. Wherever she is, wherever the Black Ship takes the souls, tell her our dream has come true.*

Someone knocked on the door.

Cerinthe took a deep breath. "Come in."

Tayla half skipped into the room. "Hello, *Miss* Cerinthe." She grinned.

"Tayla! Am I ever glad to see you. I want to thank you. If you hadn't let me in last week—"

"—you might never have been found!" Tayla finished, twirling once; several garments hanging over her arm flew out. "Here's your new uniform! And it's not grey anymore! You should've just heard Mistress Dalyrimple when I told her who it was for. Her jaw dropped so far her chins nearly splashed into the washtub, honest they did."

Cerinthe laughed.

"Can I help you dress?" Tayla asked.

"Me? No one's had to help me dress since I was three years old."

Tayla stroked the cloth. "Some of the little dainas have their own maids at home. They're used to having someone do up all their buttons in the back. The pearls let me help them. Why, what with all the different kinds of classes, they're changing clothes all day long." Tayla rolled her eyes. "That's why there's so much laundry!"

Cerinthe put on the undergarments, then a petticoat like one of the dozens she had washed. Why, she might have washed this very one. She pulled on a linen shift and then stepped into a calf-length, pearl-colored underdress. Next, came the royal blue overdress, which floated down over her head, encasing her for a moment in a rustling darkness. The skirt and sleeves tucked up to show the pearly fabric beneath. Finally, Tayla fastened the buttons—just for fun, she said.

"I've never had clothes like these." Cerinthe hitched her shoulders; she felt uncomfortable, stiff with layers. "I won't even dare to breathe."

"This is nothing," Tayla said. "You should just see what you've got for special wear, Miss Cerinthe, you should just. Real satin and brocade dresses—and silk hose instead of cotton. All provided by our very own Majesty Herself."

"For the sea's sake, don't call me 'Miss,'" Cerinthe said. "It makes me feel even stranger than I am already."

"Oh, I'd get in awful trouble if anyone heard me call a little daina by her first name."

"But we're friends."

"It's not allowed." Tayla tightened the crisp bow on her apron. "There'd be trouble for sure. And more for me than you, if you don't mind my saying."

Cerinthe sighed. "What a lot of rules they have here."

Then Mistress Blythe bustled in with a pearl comb and fastened it in Cerinthe's damp hair. "There. Now you're official. I'll take you up to your new room."

"Thanks for everything, Tayla," Cerinthe said. Tayla dropped an exaggerated curtsy and winked.

Cerinthe followed Mistress Blythe down the hall and up the grand central staircase—no more back stairs and back doors for her. As they climbed, Mistress Blythe described the school.

"Classrooms for scholarly subjects, such as reading, history, and music, are on the second floor," she explained. "Most of the dance studios are on the third and fourth floors."

Up and up they went. Students lived on the fifth and sixth floors. When they reached the south wing on the sixth floor, Mistress Blythe opened a door.

"This is the pearls' wing," she said, holding her side. "There are forty of you now, five to a bedroom, with two washrooms."

She opened another door. "And here's your room."

Cerinthe looked around. Two tiny dormer windows let in squeaks of light. Five beds lined up at precise intervals against the walls. Each bed had a low chest of drawers at the foot and a small table beside the head. One table displayed an elegant doll; her red velvet skirts draped over the edge. The second table held a fern. The next, a silver bell. On the fourth, enthroned on a golden easel, was a miniature painting of Daina Kasakol.

The fifth bed looked freshly made, and Cerinthe's canvas bag lay on the chest. Tayla must have carried it up from the smudges' quarters. Compared to that dark hole, this room seemed like a paradise. Cerinthe had just begun to read a list of rules posted on the wall—physical fights will result in expulsion; girls and boys caught alone together will result in expulsion—when suddenly doors slammed, and footsteps thundered down the hall.

Mistress Blythe smiled. "They sound more like long-shoremen than dancers, don't they?"

A bunch of girls crowded into the room.

"It's the girl! The missing girl!" several voices exclaimed.

"Hello," said Mistress Blythe. "Welcome your new classmate, Cerinthe Gale of Normost."

"No one's ever skipped aggies before," someone said, "not even Elliana."

"Doesn't look like much, does she?" somebody else whispered.

Then everyone hushed. Cerinthe saw a flash of red hair as the girls parted, making way for Elliana.

"You?" She stared at Cerinthe with her cold green eyes.

"From the gallery? All this fuss over a common snoop?" Elliana bent down and hitched up her skirt. Without shame or hesitation, she pulled off her long, frilly drawers, stepping out of first one leg then the other as everyone watched.

"Come to collect my dirty clothes?" she asked, and threw the drawers. They twirled through the air, the legs flailing, and whacked Cerinthe.

"You'll find the rest there." Elliana nodded toward a closet. "See that they are properly washed." Her eyes swept Cerinthe up and down. "Everything that comes out of the laundry here is so dreadfully dingy."

Cerinthe clasped her hands in mock delight. "Elliana! I'm so happy to see you again. Seems I was good enough after all, doesn't it?" She peeled the drawers off her skirt and hurled them onto one of the bed pillows. "I hope that's your bed? The one with the painting of Kasakol? The one right next to mine?"

Two spots like slaps of red flamed on Elliana's high cheekbones. Her eyes began their peculiar shift from sea green to sea blue.

"Mistress Blythe," Elliana said, "remove this, this…*smudge*, from my room. At once!"

Chapter Ten

But Elliana, dear," Mistress Blythe said. "This is the only free bed."

"And it's not free now," Cerinthe added, sitting down on the edge.

Elliana put her hands on her hips. "Mistress Blythe," she said, "if my parents learn that you have dared to house me with a smudge, they will withdraw their support from this school. And, as they are third cousins to the queen, they will certainly inform Her Majesty. Then you, Mistress Blythe, if you do not obey me at once, will be cast out upon the streets."

"Fishbones," said a freckled girl. "As if the queen gives three hoots where you sleep." The other girls laughed, but Mistress Blythe's fingers fluttered above her bun, making anxious little tucks and pats.

"Elliana," she said at last. "All of the students here are

considered equal. That's one reason you wear uniforms. The only thing that determines rank is ability."

"Maybe in class," Elliana said. "But not in my bedroom."

A girl pushed through the crowd, walking toward Elliana's bed, where the crumpled drawers still sprawled with one leg twisting backward. She picked them up and began to fold them.

"I'd…" she stammered, "I'd switch rooms, if you please, Mistress Blythe. That is, if Elliana will have me?"

"Ritoria." Elliana tapped her foot as she regarded the girl. "Ritoria Windsette of Inverness Bay."

Ritoria cringed like a hopeful puppy. "My family is—"

"I know everything about your family," Elliana interrupted. She turned to Mistress Blythe. "Ritoria is acceptable. Now remove that." She pointed to Cerinthe.

Halfway through her first dancing class two days later, Cerinthe was still angry at the way Elliana had snubbed her.

"Second side, pearls," called Daine Miekel, the teacher. "Remember, Isalette, the exercise is grands battements. The leg sweeps over the head, yes? Not merely to the waist."

Cerinthe turned with everyone else and placed her left hand on the oak practice barre that ran along three walls of the room. Mirrors covered the fourth.

"Ready?" Daine Miekel said. "Arms one, two…and!"

A man seated at the pianoforte, a man who seemed all bones and wrists and elbows, began to play.

Forty legs in pink hose swept up and down. Cerinthe

glimpsed herself in the mirror, one girl in a long row of girls wearing identical royal blue tunics with tight bodices and short, wispy skirts. She stole a look at Elliana. Instead of working at the barre, Elliana worked alone at the pianoforte; the place reserved for the best student in class. Her leg kicked high over her head.

Cerinthe would have hated sharing a room with "Her Highness," as the girls called Elliana. Why did Elliana dislike her so much? True, she had overheard that argument with Lady Nautilus; that might be one reason. Another might be that Elliana hated commoners. But Cerinthe had learned there were other commoners here, though not many, due to the expense of preparing for the Trial—travel, lessons, slippers, costumes. Neither reason seemed very good to her.

Concentrate, Cerinthe told herself. She was a little daina, not a smudge, no matter what anyone thought. Show them! She pointed her toe hard, turned out her feet and hips, and kept her knees as straight as masts.

"Shoulders level everyone." Daine Miekel walked down the row, giving the girls corrections. A southerner, his skin was as black and sleek as the stones Cerinthe used to find on the beach. A golden band clasped his long brown hair. Before class, he had welcomed Cerinthe skeptically—he had not been at the Trial—then assigned her a cramped corner place at the barre. Having a man for a teacher seemed strange to her.

He came closer, only two girls away from Cerinthe. Terrified, she began the battements in seconde and focused on the coiled yellow bun of the girl in front of her.

"Arm curved please, Sylva," Daine Miekel said to the girl.

Cerinthe's tongue turned drier than seaweed left in the sun. From the corner of her eye, she saw Daine Miekel glance at her, but for the third time he passed silently. Was her dancing so poor that he would not even bother to correct her?

When the music ended, Daine Miekel called, "Barre exercises are over. Stretch for five minutes, then Center Floor."

Cerinthe's tunic stuck to her sweaty back. She swung her right leg onto the barre, then slid it down the polished wood until her hamstring tightened. *Sea Maid*, she prayed, *help me. Everyone will be watching me dance. Don't let me fail in front of Elliana or the daine.*

Like a queen settling on her throne, Elliana sank into a split; her long legs seemed to stretch out forever. She arched her back, admiring her reflection in the mirror.

Cerinthe swung her left leg onto the barre and saw the ribbons on her slipper sag around her ankle.

"Center Floor!" Daine Miekel called.

While the other girls formed groups, Cerinthe hastily retied her ribbons and tucked in the knot.

"Cerinthe Gale," Daine Miekel said. "You will dance with group three. Isalette is the leader."

Isalette, the freckled girl who had scoffed at Elliana, was one of Cerinthe's roommates. She beckoned, nodding her head so that her short spiked hair waved like a sea anemone. Cerinthe ran over to her.

"Before we work on the adagio," Daine Miekel said, "I have a new assignment for you. Over the next few months, you will each choreograph your own dance."

"Stoven and sunk!" Isalette groaned. The other girls

grumbled too. Surprised, Cerinthe looked around. She had spent hours on the beach at Normost creating dances. It was easy. She simply thought about how things moved—the trees, the waves, the seals—and tried to become like them.

Daine Miekel walked over to the studio door and opened it. "Your complaints are flying outside, not into my ears. Follow them if you like, but don't come back."

The grumbling stopped.

"You will choose a theme and music," he added. "The dance must be five minutes long. Questions?"

"May we do a variation on something in the company repertoire?" Elliana asked.

"No. It must be original. Find the creative essence in yourself and transform it into dance."

Elliana frowned.

Isalette whispered to Cerinthe, "'Her Highness' couldn't put two steps together if she were sleepwalking."

"Now," Daine Miekel said, "if Isalette is through talking, we will review the adagio." He demonstrated the series of steps so quickly that Cerinthe could not remember it. She knew the class had been studying the adagio for some time because the girls simply marked the movements with their hands. "And end with the arabesque effacée into the penché," he finished. "Questions?"

Although Cerinthe had at least twenty, she didn't dare ask.

Daine Miekel nodded. "Group one, take your positions."

They did.

"Ready?" he said. "Arms one, two, and..." The slow music began.

Cerinthe watched Elliana lead group one, curious to see whether she deserved her reputation as the best dancer in class.

Expressive, confident, Elliana danced with the grace of a young priestess invoking the Goddess. Her steps were precise, yet each one flowed into the next until the adagio opened like a bud. Entranced at first, Cerinthe soon began to frown. Something was wrong, but she didn't know what. Elliana's positions were good, her carriage, her balance—all good. Then what was it?

Group one finished.

"Elliana," Daine Miekel called, "take the arabesque again please." She held the arabesque while he corrected her arm placement. "And so, and here. Your gaze follows the line of your hand. Extend! As if there were something just beyond your grasp...reach. Now lift, hold!"

Cerinthe marvelled at the difference in Elliana's appearance. Every muscle seemed alive, her body sparkling with an energy that filled the room. At last Cerinthe understood. Not once during the adagio had Elliana held or extended a position to the utmost of her ability. Now, as she lowered the arabesque into a penché, she was dazzling. Why didn't she try to dance like this all the time? If she did, she might become a famous daina someday.

"Better," Daine Miekel said. "Do you understand?"

"Oh yes, sir, I do. I do." Elliana smiled adoringly into his eyes.

"Then show me again."

She did, but her arabesque had lost its momentary sparkle; it was the same as during the adagio, lacking extension and lift. She no longer seemed to be trying.

Daine Miekel rolled in his lips and waved her away.

"Group two!" he called. As Elliana walked to the barre, she rubbed the place where he had touched her arm.

When at last he called group three, Cerinthe took a place in the back corner, knowing she could not hide, knowing that every eye in the room was on her, the new girl, the smudge who had skipped aggies. What if she danced so poorly that Daine Miekel sent her to the aggies' class? Or back to the damp dungeon? Or out of the city? Or—

"Ready? Arms one, two, and…"

For the third time, the adagio music filled the room. Cerinthe danced. The sun shining through the window soothed her body, and she lost her self-consciousness in the blend of warmth, music, and movement. So many times in her dreams she had danced at the royal school. Was she dreaming now? Was she a little daina at last?

All at once, she winced. The knot in her ribbons pinched the hollow beneath her anklebone. She had tied them too tightly. Her reverie shattered, she forgot the next step and glanced up for guidance, only to see Daine Miekel watching her. In the mirror behind him, she saw that every head was turned toward her. She fell off her arabesque and hopped to regain the relevé. Someone tittered. Rigid now, Cerinthe fumbled the penché as a second titter rippled through the room.

"Stop!" The daine clapped and the music ceased. Cerinthe hung her head, certain he was going to order her back to the laundry. And just when her hands were beginning to heal.

"Elliana!" Daine Miekel said. "Come here."

With quick, eager steps, Elliana ran to the front of the

room. "Yes, sir?" she asked and smiled her adoring smile again.

"Why have you disrupted my class?" the daine asked. "What do you find so amusing?"

"Forgive me." Elliana curtsied. "I could not help myself. You are correct, however. The situation isn't amusing but shocking. Ever since this..." she nodded toward Cerinthe "...this girl came to the Trial and then vanished, people have talked of nothing else. 'How well she must dance! How Daina Odonna wants her! The finest applicant in years!' And yet look how poorly she dances."

Cerinthe wanted to melt into the floor.

"What has happened to the standards of our school?" Elliana clasped her hands. "When a common, awkward smudge is called a protégé?"

Daine Miekel crossed his arms. "My mother was a cook. I am a commoner."

Elliana stared a moment, then tossed her head and laughed, a bit shrilly.

"You are a daine," she said, "a soloist with the royal company. Dainas and daines are members of the gentry—by royal proclamation."

"Step back, Elliana," Daine Miekel said. "Cerinthe, come forward."

"Yes, sir?" Cerinthe curtsied.

"From now on you will dance in group one, in second place. Also, during barre exercises you will work at the pianoforte— in front of Elliana."

The other girls gasped. Cerinthe felt dizzy. Did the daine honestly consider her the second-best dancer in class?

Only the group one leader was ranked higher.

Elliana opened her mouth, but nothing came out.

"You should be speechless, Elliana," Daine Miekel said. "Here is a girl who is the youngest in class and nearly as good as you. And you will have to work hard to stay ahead of her. But you don't know how to work, do you?

"You should already be with the emeralds," Daine Miekel continued. "You are older than all the other pearls." He held up one finger. "But you are lazy. Everything has come too easily. Now though, you have a challenger; you can no longer slip by on talent alone. If you want to retain first place in my class, you must learn to work. Can you?"

Her face scarlet, Elliana lifted her chin.

"We shall see if you have a dancer's heart," Daine Miekel said. "Now return to your place. Never disrupt my class again."

Elliana turned and stared at Cerinthe, her eyes angry, her head moving with an odd twitch that was something between a jerk and a shiver. Cerinthe dug her fingernails into her palms. She wished the daine had not humiliated Elliana in front of everyone; oh, how she wished he hadn't.

Now Elliana had a good reason to hate her.

Chapter Eleven

In the middle of a fouetté, Cerinthe stopped dancing; she slumped to the floor of the Wind-Rose Room, and sighed, baffled. It was Saturday afternoon. She had been trying to create a dance about the one-armed woman who sold cinnamon buns in the market, but the steps and feeling eluded her. In spite of all her efforts over the past six weeks, Cerinthe had failed to choreograph a dance for Daine Miekel.

Her stomach rumbled. The two hours after Saturday lunch were the only free time she had, so she'd skipped lunch to gain an extra hour to work. Dance classes, lessons, meals, and even etiquette lectures crammed every minute of every day, leaving scarcely a moment to breathe. Sometimes Cerinthe found a few minutes to work in the evening. But after dinner tonight, Daina Odonna had summoned the school and company to a special assembly.

Light from the windows slanted across the walls of the room, one of the gables tucked in the south wing on the seventh floor. Cerinthe had discovered it one afternoon when she had desperately needed to be alone. No one used it often because the sloping walls made it unsuitable for mirrors.

Cerinthe straightened her legs, grasped her heels, and stretched forward until her nose brushed her knee. One by one she considered new ideas for the dance. When she released the stretch, her skirt shifted. On the back was a slit the length of her thumb, not a rip but a deliberate scissors cut.

"Elliana, drat her!" Cerinthe exclaimed, slapping the floor. Ever since Daine Miekel had humiliated Elliana, she had found endless ways to make Cerinthe's life miserable. Once, Cerinthe had discovered the ribbons torn off her dancing slippers; once, waking in the morning, she had rolled onto a severed hank of her hair on her pillow; and once, she had opened her chest to find the first precious letter from her father ripped to shreds.

"Why can't Elliana just leave me alone and let me work?" Cerinthe asked the empty room. "I only want to work!"

Over the past weeks, she had worked harder at dancing than she had ever worked at anything before. The more she learned, the more she understood she needed to learn and not only about dancing. A dancer must also study art, acting, literature—everything that was beautiful. And music! Cerinthe had never danced to anything but her own voice, Tonea's humming, or the Sea Maid's glorious song.

Cerinthe let go of her skirt. Determined not to let Elliana

upset her, she stood and plunged into another idea for the assignment. She imagined she was dancing with Thordon on the deck of the *Morning Hope.* How she missed him. They had exchanged three letters, but a letter wasn't the same as seeing him. Cerinthe tried to put all her longing into the dance.

But again, she felt nothing. She stopped and wiped the back of her hand against her forehead. What if she danced without imagining or thinking anything? Danced for joy? Let the steps flow like water, as they always had on Normost?

Cerinthe did the first step which popped into her mind— glissade, jeté, assemblé, changement…then turn…pirouette, piqué, piqué—and then her mind reeled with all she was supposed to remember.

Turn out your legs from the thigh! She could hear Daine Miekel say. *Move from the center of your body. Curve your hands so they will look smaller.* Although her mind was crowded, she felt empty. *Tuck your hips. Reach!* She danced faster and faster, until she slammed into one of the angled walls.

"Stoven and sunk!" she exclaimed, rubbing her shoulder. "What's the matter with me? This used to be so easy." She sighed and looked out the window, where the sky reflected the flat pewter grey of winter. Her longing for Thordon had grown into a longing for something bigger; something that made her chest ache.

The latch clicked. The door opened, and two older girls in practice tunics came in.

"You obviously weren't listening, Sileree," one was saying. "The daina said an attitude followed the brisés volés…." She saw Cerinthe and stopped.

Cerinthe recognized Juna Wilner and Sileree Vox, the two diamonds she had seen working at the pianoforte the day she had barged into Daina Odonna's class. They were the best dancers in the school. Tall and fair, Juna had golden hair and blue eyes. Sileree was darker, with huge, bottomless eyes like a doe's and straight, brown-blonde hair like Cerinthe's.

"Well, look who's here." Juna batted her eyelashes. "I believe it's that girl who's always popping up unexpectedly. Sometimes she's a smudge in the laundry, sometimes she's first on the Trial list. And now here she is in the Wind-Rose Room, a pearl to rival 'Her Highness' they say." Juna grinned. "Where do you suppose she'll pop up next?"

Cerinthe, who didn't like being talked about as if she were not there, tapped her fingers against the window. "I didn't know this room was reserved," she said.

Sileree came and stood beside her. "Your name is Cerinthe, isn't it? How unusual. I love the way it sounds." She repeated it slowly. "Cerinthe." Her low, rich voice lilted like music.

Cerinthe smiled. She too liked the way her name sounded when Sileree said it.

"We didn't reserve the room," Sileree told her. "We come up now and then to get away."

"So do I," Cerinthe said.

"Ah-ha!" Juna did a rapid series of perfect chaîné turns, the diamond comb flashing on her head, and ended up beside them. She looked out the window. "So that's why you're here. But I wouldn't try it if I were you."

"Try what?" Cerinthe asked.

"Try to get to Kasakol's Gable from here," said Juna. "Isn't that what you were looking at?"

"I was looking at the sky."

Juna laughed. "Of course you were."

"Juna!" said Sileree. "Leave her alone."

"What do you mean by Kasakol's Gable?" Cerinthe asked. "I know who Daina Kasakol was, of course, but…"

Sileree pointed. "Three gables over, on the main wing, see where that seagull is strutting? That's where Daina Kasakol lived when she was a diamond."

"Oh." Cerinthe was awed.

"They say it's called Kasakol's Gable," Sileree added, "because she once wore a pair of dancing slippers to shreds—all in one day. So she crawled out her dormer window and hung them from the gable."

"Show-off," Juna said.

"The room's been kept just as it was," Sileree added. "A shrine of sorts. Legend says that if a little daina dances on that flat spot beside the gable, she'll become the greatest artist of her time."

"What nonsense." Juna leaned against the windowsill and stretched her calves. "The girls used to sneak out Kasakol's window to dance up there. Then twenty years ago some clumsy fool fell and broke her neck. Now they keep the room locked."

Cerinthe looked down at the courtyard seven stories below and shivered. "That's a long way to fall. Is the legend true?"

Juna snorted. "The only way to become the best is to work

hard. Throw your whole soul into it. Push yourself every single day. It doesn't matter how tired you are, or how much your feet hurt, or how much the teachers mortify you. And believe me, they will."

"Honestly, Juna," Sileree murmured.

"The child may as well learn the truth now," Juna said, "even if she is some kind of protégé from the northern wilderness or Kloud knows where."

Cerinthe frowned. "It's called the Northern Reach."

"Begging your pardon." Juna dropped an exaggerated curtsy. Cerinthe bit her lip and looked at Kasakol's Gable again. The seagull had flown away.

"Don't listen to her." Sileree put her hand on Cerinthe's bruised shoulder. "She's grumpy because Daina Odonna won't tell her why she's called the assembly."

"It must be something stupendous," Juna said, tapping the end of her nose three times. "Even the company is buzzing with rumors." She turned away from the window. "Want some advice, Cerinthe? It's easier, though still dangerous, to get to Kasakol's Gable from the roof."

"You didn't!" Sileree exclaimed.

But Juna only smiled. "Didn't what?" She walked to the middle of the room. "Now, about that variation?" She did three brisés volés and ended with an attitude. Balanced on her toe, her line fabulous, she flicked a glance at Cerinthe. "You were finished in here, weren't you?"

"Oh, yes," Cerinthe said. "Of course."

"We can go somewhere else," Sileree offered. "You were here first."

Cerinthe picked up her shawl. "No, thanks. I wasn't getting anywhere."

"I know what you mean," Sileree said. As their glance held, Cerinthe felt herself sinking into the brown depths in Sileree's eyes. The layers of color deepened from golden brown, to walnut brown, to a brown that was as dark as the bottom of the sea. Cerinthe felt uneasy; her voice caught in her throat.

"I'll look for you tonight at the assembly," Sileree said gently.

Cerinthe nodded and left the room. Instead of walking toward the grand staircase, she turned right. A short way down the hall, she turned a corner, passed two doors, and then stopped before the third. On it was a bronze plaque bearing the inscription: *Kasakol's Gable.* Cerinthe glanced around; the hall was empty. She tried the handle, but, like the longing in her heart, it wouldn't lift.

Chapter Twelve

Back in the pearls' wing, Cerinthe found the door to her room standing wide open. She approached cautiously, wondering what new trap Elliana may have laid for her, but saw only Tayla stripping sheets from the beds.

"Hello, Miss," said Tayla. "How's the new dance coming?"

"It's not." Cerinthe flopped down on her bare mattress. The sun struggled through the gray sky and shone through the dormer window.

"That's a shame," said Tayla. "I had such hopes for the one about the bun woman. I can almost smell that cinnamon." She closed her eyes and sniffed. "Delicious."

Cerinthe couldn't help smiling, but the thought of cinnamon buns made her stomach rumble—again.

"I heard that." Tayla stuffed the dirty sheets into a laundry bag. "Skipping meals isn't going to help much, if you don't mind my saying. I'm never good at my work if I've got that hollowish feeling inside."

"Can't dance on a full stomach," Cerinthe answered. She did feel hollow, but her hunger was for something more than haddock stew.

Tayla gave her a dubious glance and unfolded a fresh sheet. The feather duster tucked beneath her apron strings fluttered when she moved. Suddenly, her face lit up.

"Look, Miss." She pointed to Cerinthe's bedside table, where the sun touched the seagull's crystal wings, igniting a rainbow of colors. "He's all a sparkle! He always gives me such a friendly greeting when I come to do the rooms, but I never dust him unless you're here, Miss, not ever. Shall I today?"

"Please." Cerinthe steadied the seagull's wooden base while Tayla dabbed the duster over the delicate crystal. As the light hovered on the glass, for a moment Cerinthe saw real gulls, an entire flock swooping and careening above the sea.

The sea. The thought of it made her tired legs want to dance. Was the yearning for the sea part of her restlessness? On Normost, the sea had been a constant presence in her life. The surf had always roared, sometimes loud, sometimes soft, waking her each morning and lulling her to sleep each night. Here at the royal school, she heard only carriages and horses clattering by on the street. She had neither seen nor heard the sea since that day in the market with Thordon and—what was his name? The woodcarver. Skolla. Old Skolla.

Tayla spread a fresh sheet over Isalette's bed. Cerinthe stood up and took one end.

"Thanks, Miss, but you needn't trouble yourself." Tayla glanced at the open door.

"Let me help," Cerinthe said, "it makes me feel at home. Besides, it's easier to make beds with two people." They made three beds and started on the fourth, snapping the sheet upward until it billowed like a sail. Cerinthe stood still, watching.

Why not slip out and see Majesty Bay? She might even find Thordon down at the shipyard. Then Cerinthe sighed. She could almost hear Mistress Krissel, the housemother, say in her elegant voice: "Students who leave the school without permission and an escort will be expelled." Rule number three thousand and sixty-two.

The sun had moved; the seagull sat in shadow again. Cerinthe knew that mixed with all her other longings was the longing for her mother. The sea would not help that. Thordon would not help that. Nothing would ever help that.

Tayla tugged gently on the sheet, which had sunk into a puddle on the bed.

"Sorry," Cerinthe said. "Instead of helping you, I'm slowing you down. I was thinking about my mother—she treasured that seagull. She gave it to me just before she died."

"Oh Miss, she must have loved you lots."

"How touching," said a voice.

Startled, Cerinthe and Tayla turned toward the door.

Elliana leaned against it with her arms crossed. "Poor taste obviously runs in your family," she said. "Those knickknacks sell for five shellnars in the market. They are common glass, not crystal. Only a fool would purchase one, and only a bigger fool would actually treasure one."

Her fists balled, Cerinthe rushed toward Elliana. Instead of raising her arms to ward off the blow, Elliana merely watched, amused, with her eyes half shut. An instinct warned Cerinthe—one instilled from fights on Normost—that it was odd, unnatural, to stand so unguarded. Elliana wanted to be hit. But why? From the corner of her eye, Cerinthe saw a square of white paper gleaming on the wall—the list of rules. She stopped her swing in midair, her fist inches from Elliana's mocking face.

"Clever," Cerinthe said.

"I can't imagine what you mean," Elliana said.

"If I give you the black eye you deserve, I'll be expelled for fighting. Then you won't have to worry about losing first place in class."

Elliana yawned. "You lack subtlety. I have far more important things to do than worry about you."

"Oh? Such as eavesdropping and sneaking up on people?" Cerinthe asked. "That isn't particularly noble, 'Your Highness.'"

"What would you know about nobility?" Elliana leaned against the door again. "You don't even understand servants' etiquette. Tayla could be cast out into the street for having a student do her work—cast out without references. She would wander, penniless, starving, begging through alleys in filthy rags, and it would be all your fault."

Tayla turned as white as her cap. "Please, Miss Elliana. It won't never happen again—I swear."

"Don't worry, Tayla," Cerinthe said. "I'll explain to Mistress Blythe."

"Oh, I won't go to her," Elliana said. "I believe this is serious enough that I shall simply have to inform Mistress Odue."

Dismayed, Tayla and Cerinthe looked at each other.

"Elliana—" Cerinthe began.

"I have only your best interests in mind, Cerinthe," Elliana interrupted. "You should reserve all your strength for dancing. If you get tired, you might lose your place behind me in class. I wouldn't want that—you're such an inspiration." She smiled, looking almost shy.

Cerinthe stood, baffled. It was as if the wind had shifted, and the battleship had changed its tack. She knew it was still charging, but from which direction? Off bow or stern? From port or starboard? Any moment the ship would loom out of the fog, cannons loaded, and fire.

Elliana turned to Tayla. "I know you and Miss Cerinthe were once friends below stairs, so I can understand why you forgot yourself and stepped above your station. But that behavior cannot be tolerated."

"No, Miss." Tayla kneaded her apron.

"You're a good housemaid, Tayla, and I don't want to see you in trouble. Perhaps if you were to make this up to Miss Cerinthe?…"

"Oh, yes!" Tayla exclaimed.

"Now let me think." Elliana tapped her fingertips on her chin, then pointed to Cerinthe's practice tunic. "Look at that rip! You are so clumsy, Cerinthe. Why don't you mend that, Tayla? Just as a little penance. Then I'm certain we could all forget this little breach of etiquette."

The cannons roared in Cerinthe's ears. "Tayla doesn't have time for that," she said. "She has to work all day."

"Oh?" Elliana waved one hand. "Servants must sleep sometime or other, don't they?"

"I'll gladly do it," Tayla said.

"Marvelous. Then I won't have to mention this unfortunate incident to Mistress Odue." With that, Elliana inclined her head and walked down the hall.

Cerinthe snapped up the blanket on the bed. "This is blackmail. She ruined the dress."

"I know," Tayla whispered, trying to smooth out the wrinkles she had crushed into her apron. "Dareen down in the scullery used to work for the Nautilus family. She says Elliana was always cutting up her sisters' clothes."

"I got you into trouble," Cerinthe said. "I'll do the mending, and we'll tell her you did."

"No, Miss." Tayla grabbed her duster and whisked every inch of the doorframe. "I won't have you lower yourself by fixing anything she's ruined. Besides, she has her nasty ways of finding out, Miss Elliana does. I'll fetch your tunic when I come back to finish the beds." And with that, Tayla picked up the bursting laundry bag, tucked it beneath her arm, and marched out of the room, wielding her feather duster like a sword.

Astonished, Cerinthe sank onto her bed. How could she make this up to Tayla? The walls of the school seemed to close in. Cerinthe felt like a whale beached under the hot sun; something inside her was growing dim. She traced the seagull's wing with her finger, and the longing swept over her again, stronger than ever.

Cerinthe went to the chest at the foot of her bed and flung

it open. She rummaged frantically until she found her old cloak from Normost, then threw it on, pulled up the hood, and crept down the back stairs. When no one was looking, she slipped out a side door.

Chapter Thirteen

Cerinthe leaned against the stone wall that bordered Harbor Road and took a deep breath of the sea air, filled with the smells of salt, seaweed, and fish blowing on the southwest wind. The masts of a hundred ships spread out across Majesty Bay. Above them, eagles circled, hunting for an easy meal from floating fish heads tossed overboard. She took another deep breath and another. The sea, at last. The trapped feeling she'd had in the school eased.

Behind her, a carriage rolled by on the cobbled street. Scrolls of silver swirled along its sides and glittered on the mounted lanterns. Even the four white horses had hooves gilded with silver, which twinkled as they trotted. The carriage stopped beneath the fluttering banners over the entrance to the royal pier, where a small, three-masted pleasure ship was moored.

Its spars were embellished with gold, and Cerinthe could see the gleam of dark, polished wood. Over the ship's cutwater, the carved figure of Nemaree jutted forward with her hands cupped. Lower, her painted blue-green eyes shone on each side of the prow—as they did on every watercraft in Windward— to guide the ship safely through the archipelago.

Although the sails were furled, Cerinthe saw the tucks of blue and gold. Her father would love to make the sails for such a fine ship even though he disliked the gentry and the nobles. Spoiled and indolent he called them. It was Mama who had admired them.

"Work hard at your dancing," she had said to Cerinthe one afternoon as they cleaned the henhouse. "Become a great artist. On Faranor, even dancers who are commoners mix with the gentry. Why, you might even marry a nobleman and live in a place of beauty and grace. Ah, Faranor," Mama had sighed as she flung out another load on the pitchfork.

Now, as Cerinthe watched the people emerging from the carriage, she thought of Elliana with her noble family, beautiful clothes and home; everything that Cerinthe's mother had wanted for her. Yet, Elliana's manners would have shocked Mama. Cerinthe tugged her cloak, remembering Elliana's disdain over the seagull. How dare she make fun of Mama!

As the footman handed the last woman out of the carriage, her cloak of azure velvet rippled. Cerinthe turned away and looked out at the harbor again. The water was a more brilliant blue than any velvet cloak could ever be. She shaded her eyes, squinting toward the horizon where the sky met the sea, out where the two blues merged. At that moment, the longing hit her so fiercely that she bent double, as though someone had struck her in the stomach.

What! Why did she ache? What was she longing for? First, she had thought it was for Thordon, then later, the sea. But here were the waves slapping the seawall, and the longing was even greater.

Slowly, Cerinthe straightened. She looked along the curving line of the bay until she saw the shipyards at the far northern end. Did she want Thordon? How would she ever find him in so vast a place? Even if she did, most likely he would be working. Cerinthe huddled inside her cloak and walked toward the market district in search of Old Skolla. To make amends for the tunic, she wanted to buy a carving for Tayla.

Soon, pandemonium reigned. Wagons—stuffed with cabbages, barrels of ale, pungent spices, and rugs rolled up like fuzzy sausages—rattled past her. A musician with a basket on his head bellowed on a trumpet. Coins, dropped into vendors' hands, clinked against rings. Two fishmongers hurtled salmon and jibes back and forth, to the cheers of women in homespun skirts. "Listen to me! Listen to me!" cried a red-plumed parrot from the Southern Reach. The babble of voices grew louder and louder until Cerinthe felt like a piece of driftwood buffeted in the waves of sound, dashed this way and that.

For relief, she glanced at the fir trees on the steep, green bluff that rose to the south. Years of wind and storm had twisted them into fantastic shapes. One, as bent as an old woman, reminded her of Gwimma. They were the only trees she'd seen on Faranor that weren't planted in rows as straight as the queen's sailors.

A few blocks farther on, she spotted Old Skolla sitting by a stone wall. He looked no different than he had two months ago, as though he might even be carving the same piece of wood. His eyes flashed at her from inside the length of red wool wrapped around his head.

"Ah-ho!" he said. "The little daina has not forgotten Old Skolla after all."

"You would be hard to forget," Cerinthe said and looked down at the carvings on his mat. This time there were images of Nemaree in Her incarnations as fish mother, wise crone, and life-giving serpent. Cerinthe picked up a little dancing monkey, thinking Tayla might like it best.

"Come to buy a carving for your dancing school?" Old Skolla asked.

Surprised, Cerinthe looked at him. "How did you know I'm in the school?"

He chuckled. "The whole city knows the story of the little lost girl who was bold enough to roll up her sleeves and scrub for what she wanted. That tale's been told over many a cup of ale in this city, Cerinthe Gale of Normost. Now tell me. Has your dancing school been all that you'd dreamed?"

"I've learned a lot," she said. "The teachers are good."

"So you have, so they are. But it's true, is it not, that nothing is ever all you dream?"

Cerinthe hesitated.

"Have a seat." He nodded to a stool beside the mat. "Old Skolla smelled something brewing on the wind as soon as he saw you walking alone in your old cloak. Not what most little dainas would do. But then, you are not like most little dainas, eh?"

"I suppose not." Cerinthe sat down and rubbed the monkey's mahogany chin. "The school is all I dreamed it would be, but something's wrong. One of the girls is awful—but it's not only her. I don't know how to describe it, exactly. Something's missing."

"What do you miss?"

"Lots of things. Being alone. Being free to come and go. Normost. I miss seeing the fishing boats—*Spika* or *Long Nose* or *Sea Runner*—sail home. I would always run down to the pier to see the day's catch." She stared out at Majesty Bay, at the thicket of masts and spars and rigging. "And I miss watching my father sewing sails in his workshop. I even miss all the rain."

Old Skolla had stopped carving. "There's a name for that, exactly," he said. "Homesickness."

"No, it's more." Cerinthe put down the dancing monkey and picked up a seahorse. "Blast! Maybe I just need a good northwest wind to blow the mist from my brain or maybe a visit with Thordon."

"Northwest winds are few on Faranor. But who is this Thordon?"

Cerinthe told him.

"Hum! Hum! So that's the way the wind blows?" he said. "Perhaps Old Skolla could arrange for you to meet your friend here one day?"

"Could you!" she exclaimed. Then she frowned. "But I don't know when I can sneak away again—I'm not supposed to be here now. But I couldn't bear it anymore. I just had to see the ocean and hear it. Majesty Bay isn't quite the same as the open sea though, is it?"

"No," he said, his eyes brooding on a clipper moving out of the harbor. "Sometimes Old Skolla thinks he would like to go to sea again."

"Why don't you?"

"That time is past. Let old dreams go; let them blow. Make room for the new." He flicked a shaving from the wood. "Besides, Skolla's been so long on the sea, that the sea is in him now. No, this is the time to make my carvings and ponder many things."

A moment later, he pointed his knife at the bluff where the wind-bent firs grew. "Up on Healer's Hill there's a view of the sea that will make your soul sing."

"Healer's Hill?" Cerinthe asked.

"It's the school where the mederi train. It's a good place and free for the poor who are sick. Rich folks don't scorn it either. The best healers in all Windward are trained there."

"Don't you fear the mederi?"

"As a woman fears childbed yet delights in the babe." Old Skolla whittled away. "What is said in the Reaches is both true and not true. The mederi have magic, yes, but it comes from study and work and delving into the heart's wisdom. Real magic, that is."

"I've met Mederi Grace."

"She does much good work among the poor," he said. "Old Skolla will probably end his journey as an invalid on Healer's

Hill. Some days, bad days, I wish I'd died at sea instead of..."
he stopped.

Shivering, Cerinthe pictured the Black Ship.

"But, still and all," Old Skolla said, "there is many a thing
to be learned in the lee, before I go again to Windward."

They sat in silence until Old Skolla began to hum a sea
ditty. His knife carved, but Cerinthe could not see what was
shaping in the wood. As he sang the refrain aloud, she glanced
at the trees swaying on Healer's Hill.

> *Resolve, resolve,*
> *Howe'er the wind does blow.*
> *Come Sea Maid sing us home again*
> *From storm, from rock,*
> *Howe'er the wind does blow.*

The longing struck her again; it spread up through her
shoulders and down through her legs until it gripped her entire
body. Slowly, barely breathing, she looked at the seahorse in
her hand, then at the carvings of Nemaree on the mat.

At last she understood. She longed not only for Thordon,
or Normost, or the sea, or even her mother and father, but for
all of those and something greater still.

In all the weeks she'd spent on Faranor, she had never heard
the Sea Maid sing.

Chapter Fourteen

Cerinthe arrived back at the royal school barely in time to slip into her seat for dinner. Fortunately, everyone was chattering about the upcoming assembly, so no one had missed her. She pushed her spoon through her oyster stew, watching the whirlpools spin, dazed by what she had realized at Majesty Bay. Why had the Goddess abandoned her? What astonished her most and frightened her too was that she had taken so long to notice the Sea Maid's silence. She had been too overwhelmed by her new life.

After dinner, the students walked across the dark courtyard toward the Royal Theatre. Its windows blazed with light. Each was shaped like a nautilus shell, with swirling glass in ruby, emerald green, blue, and the brilliant violet of the sea anemone.

"I've been here for three years," said Isalette, doing a quick jeté. "And I still love going inside the theatre. It's like a magic palace."

"Is it?" said Cerinthe, barely listening. She was trying to remember the last time she had heard the Sea Maid's voice. When she stepped inside the theatre, however, she gasped. "Kloud's Bounty!"

"What did I tell you?" Isalette said triumphantly.

Cerinthe blinked. Had she suddenly stepped inside Kloud's Treasure Chest at the bottom of the sea, with all the jewels and spoils from countless ages of sunken ships? Never had she seen so much gold or imagined that so much existed in all of Windward.

Gold spilled over the tops of the white columns supporting the tiered balconies. Gold looped in filigreed garlands along the edges of the ceiling. Gold encrusted the valance, studded with mother of pearl, that crowned the stage. Even the blue velvet seats had edges of gold, and the turquoise curtain had golden fringe. Hundreds of candles burned in sconces on the walls, making all the gold glitter. Cerinthe had thought the school splendid, but it did not compare to this.

"I wish we could sit up front," Isalette said, as they edged down one of the rows of seats assigned to the pearls; only the aggies sat farther away from the stage. Near the front of the theatre, the diamonds filed into the row behind the company. The boys, their heads swiveling toward the girls, sat in the side section. Female and male students met only in partnering classes.

Sileree draped her cloak over her chair, then looked toward the back seats. When she saw Cerinthe, she smiled and waved.

Juna, who was standing beside her, waggled her finger and made a sly face.

Cerinthe waved back. The other pearls glanced at her in surprise.

"What have you been up to?" Isalette whispered.

"Nothing," Cerinthe said. "I talked to them this afternoon, that's all."

"Juna spoke to you?" Isalette clutched herself. "The dazzling Juna, the wit, the Daina's darling? If the best dancer in the school ever talked to me, I'd probably fall over dead."

"I thought Sileree was the best," said Cerinthe.

"Most people think she's only second best. Strange, isn't it, how they're such close friends in spite of being rivals."

Cerinthe sat down. How dismal that sounded—only second best. That's what she was, second best to Elliana. Cerinthe pictured a dress hanging in a dark closet during a feast, a dress with one carefully mended rip. She felt in her pocket for the carved monkey she had bought for Tayla, then leaned back and looked up at the painted ceiling. There, Nemaree embraced islands that rose amid billowing waters. To the left, Kloud blew his triton shell. A long red tendril streamed out beside it—the Sea Maid! Although Cerinthe twisted in her seat, the enormous glittering chandelier blocked all of the Sea Maid except one white hand.

Isalette nudged her. "You're squirming like an eel."

"Sorry," Cerinthe said and settled back. She stared at the outstretched hand, its palm facing forward, its fingers lifting. *Why don't You sing to me anymore?* she prayed. *I feel so empty. I have never stopped praying to You.*

"The daina's coming!" an aggie shrieked.

Daina Odonna walked onto the stage, her back straight yet supple, her black gown flowing like a thundercloud against the turquoise curtain. The man who followed her reminded Cerinthe of a hermit crab lugging its stolen shell.

"Who's he?" she whispered to Isalette.

"Daine Rexall, the head choreographer. Sour as old stockings."

When the daina faced the audience, the chatter ceased.

"I have called this special assembly," the daina said, "to quench the irresponsible rumors flying around the company and school." She looked sternly over the audience. She let them wait. "We have received a royal request," she said at last. "Queen Seaborne has requested that we create a ballet to celebrate Princess Zandora's coming of age, her sixteenth birthday, on the Eleventh Day in the Month of Greening." The daina smiled, the ruby pendant sparkling on her breast.

Everyone cheered.

Daina Odonna held up one hand; silence fell instantly. Cerinthe admired the way the daina could command the stage with a single gesture.

"This means hard work," the daina added. "The ballet—which will be called *Archipelago Princess*—will be performed in addition to our usual repertory. We shall need dancers from the school as well as the company. Six diamonds for ladies-in-waiting. A few rubies and emeralds will be needed too. And twelve pearls for the princess's Rose Court."

The pearls exploded with whispers. Cerinthe sat straight up.

"But the princess!" Elliana whispered loudly, leaning forward. "Who will dance the princess!"

"The ballet will present the highlights of the princess's life from her Naming Day to the present," the daina said. "After consulting with Daine Rexall, I have decided to use two dancers for the role. A pearl for the younger years, and a diamond for the older years."

Elliana pressed her knuckles against her teeth.

With a little shimmy of his hips, Daine Rexall stepped forward. "Daina Odonna and I will visit each class, then together make selections for all the parts. It will be a mutual—"

"Yes, yes," the daina interrupted. "The list will be posted next week. I do not need to tell you what an honor and a responsibility this is for us all. Thank you."

Everyone clapped. The theatre buzzed with voices again, much louder now, and the gold gleamed even more brightly in Cerinthe's eyes. She picked up her cloak, wondering if she had a chance for the Rose Court. Imagine dancing with the royal company!

"Who do you think will get the part of the older princess?" Isalette asked as they filed into the aisle. "Juna or Sileree?"

"Elliana will get the younger princess," Jasel said.

"I must," Elliana said in a rush, her sea-green eyes intense. "I simply must. If Daina Odonna gives me such an important role, Mother won't betroth me to—" she stopped.

"Betrothed?" Jasel exclaimed.

"Who is he?" Maiga asked.

"Poor man," said Isalette.

Elliana scowled. "Never mind."

"Come on, tell us!" the girls clamored.

Cerinthe recalled the argument she had overheard between Elliana and her mother. She scrunched up her face, seizing a chance to avenge Tayla.

"Ah…ah…ah…Mardlehop!" she pretended to sneeze.

"Lord Mardlehop!" Isalette cried, delighted. "The fattest man in Faranor!"

All the girls giggled.

"It will never happen," Elliana said, glaring at Cerinthe, "because the daina will choose me. I am the best of the pearls. And, furthermore, I am closely related to Princess Zandora."

Isalette hooted. "Since when are fourth cousins close relations? And 'furthermore,' they say the princess is kind—you couldn't possibly portray anyone kind. And 'furthermore,' maybe Cerinthe will get the part. She jumps leagues higher than you."

"If I had legs like a cart horse," Elliana said, "I could jump higher too."

Cerinthe reddened.

"Besides," Elliana added, "do you really think that Daina Odonna would insult the royal family by having a smudge represent their daughter?"

Isalette didn't say anything to that, neither did Cerinthe.

As they walked back to the school, Isalette speculated on who might be chosen for the Rose Court, but again Cerinthe scarcely heard. That lone strand of the Sea Maid's hair kept rippling in her mind, and the white hand seemed to beckon her.

Someone bumped into her back.

"Why did you stop!" the girl exclaimed.

"Sorry," Cerinthe said, "I didn't realize." She started walking again, her thoughts on fire. What if she choreographed her solo dance to honor the Sea Maid? Or, better yet, made up a dance about the Sea Maid Herself? Perhaps then, the Goddess would sing to her again. Cerinthe wanted to rush to the Wind-Rose Room and begin working, but at nine o'clock Mistress Krissel would check to see that everyone was in bed.

Long after midnight, her mind feverish with ideas for steps, Cerinthe crept out of bed. She took a candle and her dancing slippers from beneath the covers and tiptoed out of the room. Her practice tunic swished beneath her nightgown. She lit the candle from a lantern burning on the hall table, then climbed up one flight of stairs to the Wind-Rose Room.

The room was cold. Cerinthe lit three of the lanterns on the walls. Someone might notice the light—the windows had no curtains—but she wanted to choreograph the dance while the ideas burned in her mind; they might vanish if she waited too long.

When she had warmed up, Cerinthe pulled off her nightgown. She knelt on her left knee and stretched her right leg in front of her, sliding down and bending forward until her cheek touched her shin. She extended one arm and let it rest beside her outstretched leg.

There, lying flat on the floor, she recalled the sounds of the ocean: the roar like a voice humming a single, endless note; the slam of waves against rock; the quick, crackling hiss when the waves slid out to sea again. These sounds gathered and grew until at last the tide itself seemed to rise in her blood.

Accept my gift of this dance in Your honor, Cerinthe prayed, *and return to me.*

She imagined she was the Sea Maid sleeping in Her great scallop shell as it skimmed upon the dark ocean. Slowly, like a sail rising aloft, Cerinthe straightened, weaving her arms in a prolonged port de bras. She rose from her knee to her feet to her toes, susu. She moved a little faster—bourrée, glissade, balancé—hoping the flow of steps would sweep her into the dance. Instead, the shape she wanted kept flitting away, just out of reach. From the walls, the barre, the windows, it seemed to taunt her. Here! Here! No, over here! All around it she danced, pursuing, fleeing; she didn't know which. Tears filled her eyes until at last she stopped.

At least it was a feeling. At least it wasn't emptiness. Cerinthe shut her eyes, calming herself, and hummed the music she had chosen. She began over.

This time, as she crouched, two memories from the theatre sparked together: the white hand painted on the ceiling and the way a single, powerful gesture had captivated the audience. They mingled with her sadness. Cerinthe turned her hand, letting it rest on the floor with the palm facing upward.

Her fingers fluttered. Her hand lifted a few inches, then fell back again. She waited, counting imaginary swells—one, two, three—then reached toward the sky. Cerinthe rose to one knee, raised her arm, and began the port de bras. The floor seemed to vanish beneath her. Waves crested and fell, rocking the shell like a cradle, and she was the Sea Maid waking on the dawn.

The steps came. The phrasing came. The dance flowed well,

and Cerinthe knew that she had found her gift to the Goddess and her solo for Daine Miekel's class.

"What are you dancing?" a voice demanded.

Cerinthe dropped from her attitude with a thud.

Elliana stood watching from the doorway, her eyes vivid and curious, her long nightgown a slash of white against the dark hall.

Chapter Fifteen

Y ou again!" Cerinthe exclaimed, glaring at Elliana in the doorway. "How long have you been spying on me this time?" Instinctively, her hand checked the hooks on her bodice; she felt as if Elliana had eavesdropped on her prayers, and that made her feel naked. "Haven't you got anything better to do? Some scheme to plan? Somebody's clothes to cut up?"

"I was in the washroom. I saw the light from your candle and followed you." Elliana leaned forward until her heels lifted, and she stood on her toes. "Now, what is the theme of the dance?"

Cerinthe said nothing.

"If you don't tell me, I shall inform Mistress Krissel that you are sneaking around at night. You wouldn't want a blot on your record just now, would you? Not when they're trying to decide who gets to be in *Archipelago Princess*."

Cerinthe bit her lip. "It's my dance for Daine Miekel."

"Obviously. But what are you trying to express? Not a bird, or a wave, or even a ship under sail—but something like all three, with a rocking movement. Possibly something extraordinary." Her eyes made one of their astonishing changes from sea green to sea blue. "Tell me what it is!" she demanded.

Cerinthe's eyebrows raised. "Her Highness" was actually admitting that a smudge could create something extraordinary? Cerinthe started to say that the dance was her own affair, when the peculiar new expression in Elliana's eyes—a mixture of earnestness and passion—made her change her mind.

"It's someone being born," Cerinthe said.

"Who?"

Cerinthe hesitated. "The Sea Maid. She's waking in Her scallop shell and rising on the foam."

"I see!" Elliana's face lit up. "The steps are fine, fine! But you're not dancing them properly. What's the music?"

"*The Aria*," Cerinthe said, startled. "*The Aria of the Sea Maid.*"

"Perfect!" Elliana kicked off her bedroom slippers, walked barefoot into the room, and took the beginning pose on the floor. Her hair, a shock of red against her white nightgown and limbs, settled around her like seaweed, nearly covering her body. Her outstretched arm lay on the floor; the wrist fragile, the palm up.

Elliana's fingers fluttered like a trill of music, then ceased. Again they fluttered, longer, the wrist rising in delight as though surprised by the sensation of movement. Breath by breath, the Goddess awoke in the Sea Maid's body.

Her white arm swept up, tentative and joyful, the first arm reaching into the dawn of the world. Still crouched, she began to rock with the swell of the waves. Her arm fell. With a single, powerful surge, she rose to one knee, arched sideways, and for the second time swept her arm toward the sky. She began the port de bras and almost floated to her feet. The shell sailed forward. Her red hair flew out as she danced.

"Yes," Cerinthe whispered. No longer did she stand in a dim, freezing room, but in the brightness and warmth of the first sunrise the world had ever seen, witness to a miracle. Birds piped overhead; dolphins dove above the sea foam, their backs flashing silver on silver; and the rose-gold spray washed over the Sea Maid's face.

When Elliana reached the attitude, she stopped. She blinked, her pupils dilated as though part of her was still possessed by the dance.

"Don't stop!" Cerinthe cried.

"But that's all I saw," Elliana said, the rapture fading from her face. "What comes next?"

"That's as far as I got," Cerinthe said, suddenly jealous. Elliana had understood the idea and danced it not only as Cerinthe had imagined but far beyond what she had imagined. How could Elliana remember the steps so perfectly and dance them so well after seeing them only once? "You were doing fine," Cerinthe added. "Just keep dancing with the flow of it."

"But I don't know what steps come next!" Elliana cried. "Why haven't you finished this yet? Why haven't you!" She clutched a handful of her nightgown and jerked it back and forth. "I want to dance this. I tell you, I must dance this!"

Cerinthe stared, astonished, and in her confusion gave a little gulp of laughter.

"Stop laughing!" Elliana shouted. "It isn't funny. They always laughed, but it isn't funny. This is about dancing!" She spun away and stalked to the window.

"Who always laughed?" Cerinthe asked. "Do you mean the other girls? Because you can't… Because you have trouble making up dances?"

Elliana did not answer. Framed by the night, she remained motionless between Cerinthe and the window, her two heels shining like white knobs beneath the hem of her nightgown. Outside, an almost palpable darkness hid Kasakol's Gable. Cerinthe rubbed her arms, growing cold again. All the sensations of warmth and light that she had felt a moment ago had vanished. The lantern wicks needed to be turned up; their flickering flames cast tongue-shaped shadows on the walls and floor.

When Elliana turned back, whatever passion had possessed her had left, and the haughty mask had returned. Or was it a mask? Had Cerinthe just glimpsed the real Elliana?

"You are too stocky for this dance," Elliana said in her usual bored voice. "Your limbs aren't long enough. You don't have enough flexibility in your back. But my body is perfect for it. There's no question that I can dance this better than you."

Cerinthe ground the toe of her slipper into the floor. Although she was seething, she knew that Elliana spoke the truth. The dance did seem to have been made for her. But *I made it for the Sea Maid,* Cerinthe wanted to cry, for the

Sea Maid and me, not for you! It's my dance!

"If you choreograph the steps," Elliana said, "I could dance them. Then it will be the best dance it can be. Think how surprised and pleased Daine Miekel would be. And I, of course, shall still present my own dance as well."

Cerinthe cocked her head. "You want to work with a common smudge? You?"

"This has nothing to do with that! I want to dance a beautiful dance. This piece is about dancing itself, about the first movement, the divine in movement. Don't you see?"

"I never thought of that."

"If I do it, I'll learn more about dancing."

Cerinthe stared at her. Again, she felt she was seeing the real Elliana, and she liked this one better. But why didn't she feel the same fierce passion that Elliana did?

"Besides," Elliana said, "I've danced with commoners before—with the street dancers."

"Of course you have. And the moon is gold."

"It's true! When I was seven, Daina Carroll danced at our house. After that, I wanted to learn dancing—real dancing— more than anything, but my parents only laughed. 'Unsuitable,' they said. 'You may learn courtly dancing, like your older sisters. That is all you need to fulfill your role in society.'" Elliana wrinkled her nose. "So I started sneaking away to watch the street dancers. They taught me a lot."

"Didn't your parents find out?"

One of the lanterns on the wall fizzled, making the room even darker than before. Elliana stood on one leg, hooked her foot around the other, and rubbed it up and down her calf.

"Yes," she said at last. "But I didn't care. I still went. My parents were so afraid someone would find out that they gave in and let me prepare for the Trial." She laughed. "Of course I was first on the list. Daina Odonna told them I was the best applicant she had ever seen."

Elliana twisted a strand of hair around her finger. "Come. Let us put aside our differences and work together for the sake of art. That is what someone with the soul of a great artist would do."

Cerinthe hugged her arms around her chest, around the empty hollow that had begun to hurt again. The dance was never meant to be hers. It was a gift to honor the Sea Maid. If she wanted it to be the finest possible gift, shouldn't Elliana dance it?

"Decide." Elliana snapped her fingers. "I am freezing. Are you an artist or aren't you?"

"Of course I am," Cerinthe said, digging her nails deep into her palm. "All right. I agree—I guess."

Elliana smiled and twisted the strand of hair tighter. She walked to the center of the room. "Now, after the attitude?..."

Cautiously, they began to work. And *The Dance of the Sea Maid* was born on Elliana instead of Cerinthe.

Chapter Sixteen

To the dong-dong of a handbell, the priestess of the Sea Maid walked through the rows of girls and boys; over three hundred of them crouched on their heels in the school's dining hall, which had been cleared for the ceremony. It was the Day of the Dark Moon at the end of winter, when the priestess prepared the people for the Sea Maid Festival in spring. Two acolytes followed her, one chiming the bell, the other swinging a brazier. Cerinthe felt her thoughts sharpen as she breathed the vinegary, notar incense—made from a rare, holy seaweed that brought clarity to the mind.

As part of the ritual to purge the worries and fears from the dark, stormy winter, the priestess could question or bless anyone she chose, and anyone could speak to her. Cerinthe wanted to ask why she still had not heard the Sea Maid sing, even though she had been working on the dance for more than three weeks. But she feared the priestess would think her blasphemous.

"What troubles you, child?" the priestess asked an aggie.

With an awkward jerk, the aggie made the ritual response; she rose to her knees and looked up into the priestess's face. After talking to the girl, the priestess moved on. A band of white silk looped around her shoulders and hung down the front of her blue robe. On the silk, thickly embroidered in silver, were gulls, waves, scallop shells, and horned moons that glittered as she walked.

Cerinthe leaned back and felt Isalette's spine bump against her own; they each faced outward, looking in opposite directions. To Cerinthe's right and left, two more pairs of girls were sitting back to back, and this pattern repeated to form one row. A five-foot gap separated each double row of girls, creating space for the priestess to walk.

Next, the priestess stopped in front of Sileree, who neither rose from her crouch nor looked into the woman's face. If anything, she seemed to shrink. Cerinthe wiggled her fingers into the fold between her thighs and calves. Never had she seen someone fail to make the ritual response.

"I would like to hear your voice," the priestess said.

Sileree still did not look up. "So would I," she answered.

The priestess bent forward and brushed Sileree's cheek with her inner wrist, bestowing the blessing of the Sea Maid. Then she said, "In the ruins at the bottom of the sea, treasure may be found. Seek the treasure of the Goddess in your wounded soul." Behind her, the acolyte chimed the handbell twice, and the priestess walked on.

An emerald reached out. "Holy One, my mother has a lingering sickness. Will she get better?"

"Come from the sea; return to the sea. May the white swan protect her."

The procession continued down the row, around the end, and up the next row, until at last it reached the pearls. The priestess passed Isalette and Jasel before stopping beside Elliana, who had woven tiny braids into her long red curls. Elliana rose to her knees, looking up with a rapt expression. Cerinthe shifted, disgusted, although she could see only Elliana's profile. If that expression had a flavor, it would taste like those brickly-brick sweetie-sticks in the market.

"Will you stand up, child?" the priestess asked. With her usual grace, Elliana stood and then curtsied low.

"Nemaree has painted you in Her Daughter's image," the priestess said. "Tell me, how well do you dance?"

"I shall be the greatest dancer that Windward has ever known."

One corner of the priestess's mouth twitched, but when she saw Elliana's eyes change color, her amusement faded.

"Would you consider becoming a temple dancer?" she asked. "Perhaps one day, even a priestess dancer? Dedicate your art to the Goddess. What greater glory could exist for the greatest dancer in the world?"

"But Holy One, then who would know I'm great?" Elliana asked.

The priestess closed her eyes, showing their painted blue lids. "Find life beneath the surface of the waters."

Elliana watched her go, made a curtsy that was half a

shrug, and then crouched on the floor again.

The priestess neared Cerinthe, who was bursting with her question, longing to reach out her hand, to open her mouth… but the priestess passed and it was too late. A word flamed inside Cerinthe: *Mama.* Her shoulders curved around it, her chest sinking, her back rounding, as though the word were a ball that shaped her. The priestess turned. Her robe swished, swinging sideways to reveal one black foot with blue-gilded toenails before falling forward again as she stepped in front of Cerinthe.

Without thinking, Cerinthe rose to her knees and looked up, but swayed the instant she met the priestess's eyes. The incense swirled; the acolyte swung the brazier back and forth, back and forth, creating hypnotic flashes across the priestess's face. One clear, sharp thought cut through Cerinthe's mind: This look in the priestess's eyes was a thing to fear. It could change everything, could make one…what?

The priestess reached down, and the soft skin of her inner wrist brushed Cerinthe's cheek—a petal's touch, a wing's touch.

"My daughter," she said. "You already know. The answer is within you." Then she turned away.

Cerinthe sank back on her heels. Know what? What did she mean? Minutes later, or was it an hour later? Cerinthe looked up to see the priestess standing beside the head table on the dais. Her arms swept up as the handbell rang, and she made a benediction over everyone. The ceremony ended. The other students rose; only Cerinthe and Sileree remained, crouched and silent.

❊

"Balancé, arabesque effacée," Cerinthe called out the steps while Elliana danced in the Wind-Rose Room the next day. "Now drop into fourth…inside double pirouette—arms overhead, bend right…no! Wait."

Elliana stopped, her foot kicking out of a coupé, and yanked up the shoulder on her practice tunic.

"Now what?" she asked. Though they had been working for over an hour, she was not even sweating. "I danced that sequence perfectly—again. Why do you keep stopping me?"

Cerinthe fussed with a hairpin, stalling. What could she say that wouldn't push Elliana's anger over the edge? "Try to put more into the steps," she said.

"That explains nothing."

"Well, after the pirouette, for example, bend from your waist only and reach into the stretch as far as you can. Pretend something's pulling you toward it. Like this." Cerinthe demonstrated.

This was their fifth practice session for *The Dance of the Sea Maid*, and it was nearly complete, complete but not polished. That extra tilt of the head, that lingering sweep of the arm, that elongation of the leg through the pointed toe—all of which gave a dancer tension and brilliance—these eluded Elliana. Today more than ever.

"Try again," Cerinthe said, "from the phrase in the aria, 'We honor your unfathomable gifts, oh Sea Maid risen from the deep…'"

With her legs as stiff as stilts, Elliana walked mincingly on pointe to the corner and began to dance, one arm twitching like a sole caught in a net. After the arabesque effacée, she spun into a wild, out-of-control triple pirouette, then bent from the waist, and fell hard without having stretched at all.

"Skulls and skullduggery!" Elliana slapped the floor. Cerinthe rolled her foot up and down, trying not to grin; Elliana had learned several colorful curses from her.

"You just have to work at it," Cerinthe said. "Try again."

"Try! Try! Try! That's all anyone ever says to me. Daine Miekel. Daina Odonna. Try, Elliana. Work, Elliana. I'm weary to death of it!"

Halfway between heel and point, Cerinthe's foot froze.

Elliana flopped onto her back and lay on the floor in a sloping rectangle of light from the window. The leaded wrought iron that separated the panes cast a shadowed grid over her body; the blurred, crisscrossed lines shifted with every breath she took.

"Mother found out that the priestess asked me to join the temple," Elliana said suddenly. "She wants me to accept, because 'it would be invaluable to have a high priestess in the family,'" Elliana mimicked her mother's voice. "And a few hours ago, Daina Odonna told me she will not intervene unless I prove I can work."

"No wonder you can't concentrate," Cerinthe said, but she was imagining the school without Elliana, life without Elliana. How wonderful it would be to wake each morning, to turn each corner, without expecting someone to pounce.

"I shall never join the temple, never. I shall do something so abominable the priestess won't..." Elliana sat up, glaring. "I know. I'll eat dolphin flesh."

"You can't! You wouldn't."

"I would. I'll do anything to be a dancer—a real dancer." White flecks bubbled in Elliana's eyes as they turned from blue to green. "I have to learn to work harder, but not only because of the temple. It's the only way to become the greatest dancer in Windward."

Cerinthe stared. "Learn to work harder?"

"Dancing has always been easy, until lately," Elliana added. "Everyone is right; I don't know how to work hard. But you—" she stood up. "You're a commoner—born to work. Show me how."

"Me?"

"Please," Elliana said, with the same earnest expression that Cerinthe had glimpsed that first night in the Wind-Rose Room. Was she in earnest though? Or was she using her earnestness as a form of cunning? All of her life, Elliana had obtained everything through tricks and stratagems. But now, for the one thing she really wanted—to dance well—that was not enough.

Cerinthe's toes cramped, strained from being flexed for too long. Inch by inch, she lowered her foot. If she taught Elliana to work, she would give up her only advantage. Why should she? With Elliana gone, she would be the best dancer in the class. As Cerinthe stared down at her foot, she noticed the neat little tuck in her tunic, the rip that Tayla had mended. Cerinthe remembered how Elliana had almost tricked her into starting a fight so the school would expel her, leaving Elliana to reign supreme again.

"Well?" Elliana asked.

Cerinthe frowned. If she could succeed only by having Elliana leave, then she was as pathetic as Elliana. That kind of success would be as sour as pickled oysters. Also, Cerinthe now recognized the earnest expression in Elliana's eyes: She could name it; she could touch the place on her own chest that harbored the same emotion—longing.

"Two hours," Cerinthe blurted. "I'll spend two hours helping you." But how would she teach Elliana to work? Her teachers had tried; Daina Odonna had tried, and all their praise and threats had failed. Cerinthe looked out the window at the sloping gable not far away. Then she thought of the portrait beside Elliana's bed.

"Follow me," Cerinthe said. She walked out of the room, down the stairs, and into the Gallery of the Great. There, she stopped beside Kasakol's statue, which had a crack zigzagging through the marble knee.

"Is this what you want more than anything in the world?" Cerinthe asked Elliana, nodding at the statue.

"Yes, but—"

"Then face it, and stand in first position."

Elliana did.

"Lead with your heel," Cerinthe said, "and tendu front. Point your toe toward the statue—toward the thing you want more than anything."

Elliana pointed.

"Now back to first," said Cerinthe. "Again. Point harder! Point as hard as the thing inside you that wants it. Point as hard as the wanting, the longing." Her voice wavered. "The longing is in your foot, your foot reaching toward what you want."

All of Elliana's power, all of her energy poured through her leg and beamed out through her toe toward Kasakol's statue. Her leg almost hummed: taut, brilliant, beautiful. After the fourth tendu, a tiny drop of sweat ran like a tear down her cheek.

Chapter Seventeen

One evening ten days later, just after the bell tolled seven, Cerinthe sat on her bed reading a history book when Isalette poked her head in the door.

"Cerinthe!" Isalette said. "Didn't you hear the commotion?"

"What commotion?"

"The list of parts for *Archipelago Princess* was just posted in the Grand Entry! The whole school's probably down there by now. Put that book away and let's go see."

"No," Cerinthe said, picturing the throng of girls, each hoping to see her name on that wonderful, terrible list. "I have to…go work on my dance in a few minutes. Besides, I'm sure Elliana got the part."

"Oh, fishbones on Elliana! Aren't you wild to know?"

"I already do," Cerinthe said, a fluttery feeling in her stomach. "Remember what happened when Daina Odonna came to watch class?" Elliana had looked like a princess and danced like a princess; after all, she was noble, and it showed in every gesture. How could a common island girl possibly compete with that? The class and the waiting, worrying, and hoping that followed, had felt like the Trial all over again. As Cerinthe turned a page she had not read, she realized that this would always be part of a dancer's life. Even if she became a daina one day, the head of the company would always decide whether she danced a part or not. That troubled her.

"Elliana will be a perfect princess," Cerinthe said, turning another page.

"You're hopeless." Isalette leaned against Cerinthe's bed. "I'll wager you three shellnars that you've been chosen to be the princess—and a rose too." She grabbed the history book.

"Give it back!" Cerinthe exclaimed.

But Isalette held the book behind her. "Cerinthe Gale," she said severely, "don't you remember what happened the last time you didn't bother to see a list?" She grinned.

Cerinthe had to laugh. "Yes. I made a mess of everything."

"Come on then!" Isalette laid the book beside the seagull on the bedside table, grabbed Cerinthe's hand, and pulled her into the hall. They ran down four flights of stairs. On the last flight, between the first and second floors, they heard feet thundering up and voices clamoring.

"Where is she?" a girl cried.

"And where's Elliana gone?" someone else shouted.

"Cerinthe! There's Cerinthe!" At least fifteen pearls clustered on the stairs below. "Cerinthe!" they shouted. "You're to dance the young princess!"

She clutched the banister.

"Kloud's Bounty!" Isalette shouted. "I told you! I told you! Let us through, girls, so she can see for herself."

Cerinthe felt dizzy, but Isalette dragged her down the last flight of stairs. Students jammed the Grand Entry, some talking and laughing, some crying, like the ruby who had collapsed on one of the priceless brocade chairs. Her red underskirt caught around the armrest and bunched up like an accordion. "Get up!" Another girl shook her. "Hurry! Before Krissel spots you."

Isalette barreled through the crowd, forging a path straight to the golden easel. Cerinthe followed, her head throbbing. What if the girls were having a joke at her expense, urged on by Elliana?

A stiff piece of parchment hung on the easel. Cerinthe skimmed the calligraphy until she found:

The Role of Her Royal Highness, The Princess Zandora
Older Princess: Sileree Vox of Umbrea
Understudy: Juna Wilner of Alicia
Younger Princess: Cerinthe Gale of Normost
Understudy: Elliana Nautilus of Faranor

"There!" Isalette said. "Three shellnars please."

Cerinthe blinked. It was true. Farther down the list, she saw her name written again under the roses. Two parts? She read them over and over until an emerald finally pushed her aside, saying, "So now that you're a star you won't let anyone else have a look?"

Dazed, Cerinthe moved away. On the far side of the room, the diamonds clustered around Sileree, who stood quietly accepting congratulations. She looked tired; the skin around her eyes had an odd, olive pallor. Juna chattered gaily beside her. Anyone would have thought that Juna had been given the part, and Sileree was the understudy.

When Sileree saw Cerinthe, the corners of her mouth lifted. Their eyes held, and again, like the day in the Wind-Rose Room, Cerinthe felt some wordless understanding pass between them. She still didn't know what it was.

"It doesn't seem fair," a pearl complained behind her, "that Cerinthe gets two parts when some of us don't even get one."

Cerinthe scratched her cheek and looked down at the carpet; she knew how awful if felt to be left out.

"Why, in the Sea's name, did Daina Odonna choose Cerinthe instead of Elliana?" an emerald asked.

"Because Cerinthe's shorter and..." someone began. Cerinthe strained to hear more, but Ritoria pounced on her.

"Cerinthe! Kloud's Bounty to you!" Ritoria's cowlick curved straight up. Then the rest of the pearls surrounded Cerinthe. A few of the rubies and emeralds congratulated her too. She saw envy in many faces, and some of the girls clasped her hand too tightly. Something inside of her shrank back.

"I can't wait," Jasel said, her eyes dreamy. "Rehearsal with the company in the Royal Theatre." She had been chosen to be a rose.

"Has Elliana been down?" Isalette asked.

Jasel nodded.

"Whatever did she say?" Ritoria asked.

"Nothing at first," Jasel said. "She looked at the list for the longest time and didn't twitch so much as a muscle. Of course, everyone was watching her. Then she said that her parents were fetching her for a party, and she had to dress."

"She always says that." Maiga giggled. "But only her mother comes to visit—and only when she's in trouble. I've never seen her father or her nine older brothers and sisters; she's the youngest. True, the carriage comes but only with two footmen."

"Maybe she makes up all those parties." Jasel shrugged.

"At least she's a rose," Isalette said. "She ought to be satisfied with that. I'd be too nervous to dance in front of the queen and king myself. You know me—I'd trip over a stage light, and the theatre would go up in a blaze." Isalette was a rose understudy.

Even as Cerinthe put one arm around her friend's shoulders, she felt shocked. The queen and king! Until this moment, she had forgotten that she would be dancing before them and a thousand other strangers as well.

"Are you all right, Isalette?" she whispered, sensing her disappointment.

"Fine as figs."

"Then I'm going back to our room." Cerinthe wanted to be alone. She wove through the crowd and climbed slowly up the stairs.

"Oh Mama!" she whispered. "I'm to dance the princess. How pleased you would be. I wish you knew." At least her father and Thordon would know; Cerinthe could hardly wait to send them the news. With every step, she felt more ecstatic, more terrified and stunned. But she also had doubts. Had Daina Odonna chosen her merely because she was shorter than

Elliana? And how could the daina think Elliana would ever consent to be her understudy?

On the sixth floor landing, where Cerinthe turned toward her room, a red-gold fish darted inside the aquarium. She stopped, realizing she was late for her practice session with Elliana. The picture of a furious, screaming Elliana filled her mind. They had only a minute of the dance to complete, but Cerinthe suspected that now their shaky partnership would end. She wasn't sorry. A bubble swelled through the hairgrass in the aquarium and popped on the surface of a crimson lily. She was still jealous that Elliana danced the Sea Maid with such grace, as though the Goddess Herself came and dwelled in her body, inspiring each lift of the hand, each tilt of the head, each gliding step. It wasn't fair.

Sea Maid, Cerinthe prayed. *I created the dance. Why don't You come to me? Inspire me?*

She changed into her tunic and then climbed on up to the seventh floor. If Elliana was quitting, Cerinthe needed to begin practicing the dance immediately. Besides, she had to face Elliana's rage sometime.

When she reached the Wind-Rose Room, it stood dark and empty. The angled roof seemed to crash into the walls; even in the gloom the white trim separating them glimmered like a raised cord. Elliana would not be coming; she must have gone to a party after all. Cerinthe's hands uncurled, not quite relaxing, and she walked cautiously into the room. She shook her head, scoffing at herself. There was nothing to fear. Besides, now she could perform the dance herself, as she had always wished. The offering, the gift, was completely hers again. As she turned to leave, a flash leaped out of the darkness. She jumped back. No one was there.

Across the roof, on the southern wing, light glowed in the third window—a window where she had never seen a light before. It flickered on and off, as if someone paced before a candle. Cerinthe left the room, walked down the hall, and stopped beside the closed door to Kasakol's Gable, where a broken yellow line gleamed along the threshold. Someone was inside.

Cerinthe raised the cold latch, making it clink, and opened the door. In the dim candlelight, she saw the window on the far wall. A huge iron bar hung across it, bolted on each side and fastened with padlocks. No one could get onto the gable roof that way, not even by breaking the glass; the panes were barely the width of two hands.

To her left, a single bed threw an oblong shadow over the floor—a shadow cast by the candle burning on the table in the corner. The bed pointed toward the window. On the floor, leaning against the footboard and looking out at the night, sat Elliana. Some of her hair had slipped from its bun and swooped over her neck. Wherever her skin showed through, the candlelight turned it the color of old lace. She did not look around even when Cerinthe shut the door.

"How did you get the key?" Cerinthe asked, braced for an outburst. But Elliana said nothing. Her silence and a smell like clams spoiling in the sun—a smell that made Cerinthe quiver—filled the room.

"Does this mean you won't be doing the Sea Maid's Dance?" Cerinthe asked.

"I wouldn't dance your stupid dance in front of Daine Miekel for all the gold in Windward," Elliana said. "Not if Kasakol herself begged me to. I swear on her grave."

Cerinthe relaxed; this was the Elliana she knew. Almost against her will, though, the fetid smell drew her forward. Step by step, she walked farther into the room until she saw Elliana's legs illuminated in a triangle of light. They stuck straight out in front of her, slack, turned outward from years of dancing. Her skirt hitched almost to her knees, revealing the muscled white calves. Lower, lying nearly sideways against the floor with the heels together, were her feet....

"In Nemaree's name!" Cerinthe cried. "What happened?" All over Elliana's feet, blisters swelled—some bulging, some oozing pus, others crusted with blood or scabs. They covered her toes, the bottoms and sides of her feet, even her heels. Cerinthe clapped her hand over her nose. She had known, known the instant she entered the room, that the fetid smell came from a putrefied wound.

"You," Elliana said, her voice toneless. "All I ever wanted... is gone because of you. A common stinking smudge. Why didn't you stay in your wattle hut? I should be the princess, and you know it."

"Maybe," Cerinthe said.

"I can't believe how I lowered myself. Working with you. Asking you to teach me to work. It sickens me. Work! I did work." She pointed to one bloody foot. "See? And what good did it do? Nothing."

Cerinthe winced. "You should go to the dispensary."

Elliana laughed. "Oh, this is nothing. See these scars?" She touched the raised, crisscrossed white lines on her arch, one of the few places without blisters. "Whenever I came home after running away to see the street dancers, Nanny would whip my feet. Whip them and whip them with a leather thong."

Speechless, Cerinthe shivered.

"But did I let that stop me? No!" Elliana's voice grew shrill. "I won't stand in anyone's shadow again. Nothing will ever stop me from dancing. Not my mother, not the priestess, and certainly not a smudge. Do you want to know what happened to Nanny?" She laughed wildly. "Oh it wasn't pleasant; it wasn't pleasant at all. You had better watch out, Smudge. Grow eyes in the back of your head. Because I swear I'll lash you to a rock and dance on the beach while the tide comes in."

Cerinthe backed up.

"That's right," Elliana said. "Run away, run away; but it's too late, it's already too late for you." And she turned her head toward the dark window again.

Cerinthe stumbled from the room. In her hurry to escape the silence and the fetid smell, she left the door open. As she ran down the stairs, the smell seemed to run with her, to catch at her, to tear in her throat, trying to make it as raw as those blistered feet. They swelled in her mind, growing bigger and bigger until they became monstrous—sea monsters. What kind of girl could be attached to such feet, could endure such torment....

Cerinthe's own bedroom door stood wide open. A dozen chattering girls crowded inside, some jumping up and down to see over the backs of those in front.

"She's here," Maiga said. All the girls turned, looked at

Cerinthe, and then stepped aside. Tayla knelt on the floor beside Cerinthe's bed, surrounded by a thousand sparkling fragments of glass. Cerinthe looked at the bedside table; the history book was still there, but the crystal seagull was gone.

Tayla twisted toward her. Tears streaked her face.

"Oh Miss," she sobbed. "I just came up to turn down the beds, and I found him here all broken everywhere, and he that was so beautiful!" Tayla wadded her white apron.

Cerinthe crossed the room and knelt beside her. The seagull's fragments looked almost powdery, as though after they had been broken, someone had ground them into even smaller pieces.

Tayla sobbed harder. "Who would have done such a wicked thing? Perhaps a cat got in."

The door creaked. Mistress Odue strode in and towered over Tayla. "I'll know the meaning of this, you chit; I'll know the meaning! Explain yourself this instant."

"I—"

"Dishonoring Her Majesty's institution!"

"It was an accident," Cerinthe said. "Tayla didn't do it."

"Oh yes she did—and on purpose, too." Mistress Odue snatched off her gold-rimmed spectacles and wagged them in Tayla's face. "Elliana saw her."

Chapter Eighteen

In spite of all Cerinthe's protests, and Tayla's repeated cries of, "No, I never touched him! Never! He was that beautiful!" Mistress Odue believed Elliana's story.

"Blundering servants are not tolerated in Her Majesty's school," Mistress Odue told Tayla. "And as for lying ones!…" Her pointed collar snapped up and poked her chin. "I should turn you out into the street." She grabbed Tayla's arm and dragged her away.

For half the night, Cerinthe tried to sleep, turning from side to side until her anger and sadness jumbled together like the blankets on her bed. She knew Elliana had broken the seagull in revenge; Elliana had a talent for striking where it would hurt most.

"I've lost my last piece of Mama," Cerinthe whispered under

her pillow. She was beginning to think Elliana capable of anything. *I'll lash you to a rock and dance on the beach while the tide comes in....*

...drowning. Cerinthe was drowning. Black water swarmed in her throat, in her eyes, in her nose. Bubbles streamed up, popping, then fading into silence as she sank. Two white sea-monsters charged, their bloody tongues lashing from side to side....

Gasping, Cerinthe woke and pushed her pillow away from her face. Across the room, daylight shone through the dormer window. Isalette snored in the next bed. Cerinthe took a few deep breaths to shake off the nightmare, then dressed, threw her old cloak around her uniform, and pulled up the hood. She crept down one of the servants' back stairs. Surely Mistress Blythe would tell her what had happened to Tayla.

In the basement hall, Cerinthe hunched her shoulders and shuffled, trying to look like a humble job seeker. Little dainas were not allowed downstairs anymore than smudges were allowed upstairs. "Everyone has her place and should be in it," Mistress Krissel always said. Two upper housemaids bearing silver trays with covered plates and steaming pots of chocolate approached Cerinthe. The smell of buttered toast filled the air.

Cerinthe bobbed a curtsy and stepped aside. With taffeta crackling and silver spoons clinking against little dishes of jam and butter and honey, the upper housemaids swept past. Cerinthe ran toward Mistress Blythe's door, but just as she reached it, the door opened. Voices spilled out. Although Mistress Blythe would probably not betray her, someone else might.

Opposite the door was a laundry cart piled high with folded towels. Cerinthe ducked behind it.

"Thank you for looking at Lisanne," Mistress Blythe was saying. "I didn't know what to do. She screamed all night—half hysterics, I think."

"You were right to send for me," a woman answered.

Cerinthe frowned, trying to place the familiar voice.

"A torn hamstring." Mistress Blythe sighed. "I told her to rest after she pulled it last week, but she kept on working until it ripped."

"Lisanne is young," said the woman. "She should mend well, but it will take care—and rest."

It was Mederi Grace. Cerinthe pressed her cheek hard against the towels on the bottom shelf.

"It's been one injury after another lately," Mistress Blythe said. "These children push themselves too hard. Poor Lisanne, she may never catch up. This is exactly how so many of the students lose their places here. They won't rest long enough for their injuries to heal. And if you want my opinion," Mistress Blythe lowered her voice, "the teachers don't help. I'm at my wit's end."

"These children simply must have a mederi or a healer in residence," Mederi Grace said. "What if there was a crisis? The queen's minister of charitable institutions could authorize one, but he is always too busy to see me. I promise to keep trying."

"Thank you."

"By the way," Mederi Grace said, "how is Cerinthe Gale getting on?"

Cerinthe's eyes widened.

"Brilliantly," said Mistress Blythe. "She's been chosen to dance Princess Zandora in the new ballet."

"Indeed? Anything else?"

"Her teachers say that she seems rather sad occasionally. Homesickness, most likely."

"Perhaps." Mederi Grace sounded doubtful. "I'd like to speak with her sometime."

Why? Cerinthe's cheek was beginning to itch from the rough towels. The acrid smell of the laundry soap, a smell that she remembered all too well, filled her nose.

"May I ask your advice on another matter?" Mistress Blythe asked. "Last night, Mistress Odue demoted one of our most promising under housemaids to the laundry."

No! Cerinthe clutched one wheel on the cart. Not the dungeon for Tayla! Tayla without her crisp black and white uniform? Tayla, a smudge?

"How may I help?" Mederi Grace asked.

"The poor girl has weak lungs, and the washroom is terribly damp. Is there any medicine I can give her to prevent sickness?"

"Come with me to the dispensary—I need to return this book and check on the proturra supply. I'll tell you what symptoms to watch for."

Keys jingled as Mistress Blythe locked her door. Cerinthe scrunched into a ball until the two women passed her hiding place. After they turned the corner, she darted off in the other direction, toward the central staircase. Cerinthe ran up the steps two at a time, pulling off her old cloak and wadding it under her arm as she ran. When she reached the main floor, she forced herself to slow down by chanting "ocean" between each step. By the fifth floor that had changed to "Tayla—Tayla—Tayla."

The bell struck eight, time for breakfast, but Cerinthe knew she could not eat. Her rage grew stronger with every gong. Tayla in the dungeon! The seagull broken! And all because Elliana was jealous. All because of a part in a ballet. Storm and thunder!

Up in the Wind-Rose Room, Cerinthe kicked off her shoes and grabbed the barre. She did a plié, straightened, rose to her toes in a relevé, and then bent her knees in another plié. Over and over she repeated the exercise—five relevés, ten, fifty. How could she help Tayla? How could she prove that Elliana had broken the seagull? Cerinthe paused on her toes. The mederi wanted to speak to her. If she explained about the seagull, would the mederi use her influence to help Tayla?

Why not go down to the dispensary and ask? Cerinthe felt her ankles wobble. She hadn't been in the dispensary since the day she had fled from the glimroot, and she didn't want to be there now. Yet, part of her wanted to hear the mederi's advice about weak lungs, wanted to see the mederi's serene brown eyes again.

Cerinthe walked to the window and looked out, yearning for the Sea Maid. *You who ride the waves from the Islands of the Blessed, send me strength*, Cerinthe prayed. *Fill me with Your voice when I dance. Help me to help Tayla.* But the Sea Maid remained silent. The slates on Kasakol's Gable shone with a grey reflective light, the color of the sea at home on an overcast summer day. Cerinthe felt like a lost sailor clinging to the mast of her capsized ship. Away on the horizon, Mederi Grace seemed to burn like a distant light.

"I won't go inside the dispensary itself," Cerinthe decided. Instead, she would ask the mederi to come out into the hall.

Minutes later, Cerinthe paused on the threshold of the dispensary. The door was open.

"Hello?" she called, scraping her nails against her palm. No one answered. All of the sickroom doors were closed, but she sensed that something or someone—probably Lisanne waited behind one of them. The white curtains still hung at the windows, and the blue-and-white jars still…Cerinthe looked away.

"Mederi Grace?" she called louder. "Please, can I talk to you?" She let out a long breath, half-relieved that the mederi had already gone.

Two steps away from the door, a thick, magnificently bound book sat on a chair. A gold medallion shone on the green cover, which was tooled with leaves and flowers fashioned of tiny pieces of colored leather. The edges of the pages were silver.

Never had Cerinthe seen such a beautiful book; it had to be the work of a master binder. She stepped over to the chair. Across the top of the book, the words *Leigh's Herbal* were embossed into the leather. On the medallion, engraved in fine lines, a serpent coiled around a scallop shell and open hand— the healer's symbol. The medallion was a fancy version of the clay healer's charm that Cerinthe had tossed into the courtyard fountain. Suddenly, she trembled, fighting the treacherous riptide that swept her toward grief.

Stay at the bottom, she wanted to shout. I threw you away. Stay at the bottom! Furious, she picked up the book, sat down, and plunked it on her lap. She hooked her heels over the bottom rung of the chair and randomly opened the book.

A burst of color startled her eyes. The word, "Delamin," outlined in cobalt blue and filled with red and gold, decorated the top of the page. Below, intricate illustrations of the plant showed sections and cross-sections. The text described the herb's medicinal uses, and notes in the margin gave details about growing and harvesting.

The faint pink of her fingertips slid under one thin, white page after the other. She read faster and faster, shocked by how few herbs she knew and by how little she knew about them. When she reached giress in the "g" section—the *Herbal* was arranged alphabetically—she learned that an infusion of giress and wild oats could relax the nervous system. Gwimma had never taught her that.

Then Cerinthe read: "Never use giress to cool a fever, for it may cause fatal heart palpitations." Horrified, she looked up. Gwimma had always used giress for fever; she could have killed someone. Maybe she had.

No sound broke the stillness in the dispensary, not a rustle, not a voice, not a single creaking board. The sickroom doors seemed to stretch taller and wider, as though something waited behind all of them now, something bursting to get out.

Cerinthe rubbed her fingers over the silver-edged pages; they felt smooth. Why had Gwimma scorned book learning? If they had owned an herbal, Cerinthe might have saved her mother's life. "You should never have used the glimroot," Gwimma had said. Could she have been wrong about that too? Maybe she hadn't known how to use the root properly.

Cerinthe turned the next page, page fifty-two, and saw the word "Glimroot" written across the top.

"No!" she exclaimed, slamming the book shut. Tears sprang into her eyes. She could not bear the thought that she might have been able to cure her mother but had been too ignorant. She jumped up. She was an ignorant, common girl from an obscure island on the edge of the kingdom, and she didn't know anything! Not anything! She could not help Tayla or anyone else.

On the cold stage of the Royal Theatre, Cerinthe danced the chassés in the "Rose Variation" with eleven other pearls and tried not to cry. If Daine Rexall started shouting at her again, she would burst.

The last six weeks had passed in a flurry of rehearsals for *Archipelago Princess*, but this was the first one in the theatre. No scenery brightened the stage; instead, black curtains hung down on each side, creating wings where the dancers made entrances and exits.

"No, no!" Daine Rexall called. The music stopped. The pearls stopped dancing. "Cerinthe Gale!" he exclaimed. "Stay in line. Dance in unison with the others. I've stopped the rehearsal three times to tell you. Have you no brain?"

No, Cerinthe wanted to shout, I don't! But she said, "I'm trying."

With a wounded expression, Daine Rexall pressed his fingertips together, making a triangle with his hands.

"All of the roses in the Rose Court form an exquisite bouquet," he said and tapped his thumbs. "As though each stem has been plucked from the same carefully cultivated bush." His thumbs tapped again. "Anyone who stands out destroys my artistic impression." Tap. "Ruins it." Tap, tap. "Devastates it."

Cerinthe wanted to hide behind one of the black curtains.

"If you continue to traipse around like a blowzy rose," Daine Rexall added, "I will replace you."

Elliana tittered.

"Such a drastic step would hurt me as much as you, Cerinthe," Daine Rexall said, "but it would be for your own good. You must learn. Now don't force me to take that step."

"I won't, sir," she half-whispered.

"From the beginning." Daine Rexall waved his arms.

This time Cerinthe mimicked Jasel, who was dancing in front of her as stiffly as a puppet. She refused to give Elliana or anyone else the satisfaction of seeing her fail. Now more than ever, Cerinthe dreaded the afternoon rehearsal, when she would have to dance her solo in front of everyone. Even Daine Rexall had not seen her perform it yet; his assistant, Daina Lizabrina, had taught her the steps. Elliana had refused to be her understudy in spite of dire warnings from Daina Odonna.

Now, leading the roses, Elliana extended her leg in a sloppy développé. Cerinthe thought of those oozing blisters and marvelled that Elliana could dance at all. After losing the princess part, her spurt of hard work had ended; she was lazier than ever before. Her mother's purple carriage had been parked in the courtyard twice this week; unmistakable with its fretwork of golden nautiluses over the wheel hubs.

During lunch, Cerinthe sat quietly in the dining room with the other pearls. She turned her plate a quarter turn, then another quarter turn, and watched the steam escape from the tiny holes in her pork pie. To take her mind off the rehearsal, she tried to think of another way to sneak into the laundry. Each of her three attempts to see Tayla had failed.

"Oh Blowzy Rose!" Elliana called from across the table, a few seats down from Cerinthe. "Pass the sugar. But no thorns, if you please."

Cerinthe hesitated, then passed the salt instead. This was the first time Elliana had deigned to speak to her since destroying the seagull. Nothing else had happened, but Cerinthe didn't believe for a moment that Elliana was finished carrying out her threats.

"Just what is a blowzy rose anyway?" Maiga asked.

"From looking at our precious smudge here," Jasel said, "I would guess it's a rose with a great big fat red face."

The three girls giggled.

Cerinthe picked up her fork, stabbed the pork pie, and cut it in half.

"I believe," Elliana said, "that a blowzy rose is the kind of coarse, straggly object one frequently observes on a slattern's hat."

Cerinthe speared half the pie and flung it across the table. It splattered against Elliana's chest, spewing out chunks of pork and splashing all three girls with brown gravy and peas.

"How dare you!" Elliana screamed. The other girls screamed too.

Cerinthe fled.

When the rehearsal resumed two hours later, Cerinthe pinned a shawl over her practice tunic; the Royal Theatre was still cold. She held onto a ladder in a corner and warmed up, finally finishing with grandes battements. Out on the stage, beneath chandeliers which cast tear-shaped flickers on the floor, the company dancers also warmed up; they held portable barres.

Daina Carroll, who was dancing the queen, practiced grandes battements too. The difference between her battements and Cerinthe's was like the difference between a glowing harvest moon and a wan quarter moon. Cerinthe rubbed her hands together to stop them from shaking.

Sea Maid, she prayed, *You who sail the sea where the earth meets the sky, give me the courage to dance in front of these great dancers. Let me hear Your voice and feel Your presence again.*

"Act One, Scene One," called Daina Lizabrina. "'The Naming Day.'" The stage hands removed the portable barres.

During Scene One, Daina Carroll danced with a doll dressed in a white lace gown. Cerinthe, waiting backstage to open Scene Two, cringed whenever Daine Rexall stopped the dancers. An hour later Daina Lizabrina came over to her and said, "It's almost time for your cue."

"I can't…" Cerinthe pressed her hand to her mouth. "In the name of Nemaree—I'm going to be sick!"

Daina Lizabrina patted her arm. "It's only stage fright. Come along. I'll show you where to stand in the wings."

Cerinthe rubbed her slippers in the golden resin and heard it crunch. She took her preparatory position. In the shadow of the black wings across the stage, Sileree waited too, looking grim. Cerinthe danced the princess in only one scene, then Sileree replaced her.

The opening notes of the honey-sweet melody rippled on the pianoforte. Terrified, Cerinthe danced onto the stage—four chassés, piqué, piqué…

"You're late!" Daine Rexall called. The music ceased. Cerinthe stopped, the muscles tightening along her neck and shoulders. She couldn't bear much more of this. Voices muttered, and to Cerinthe's surprise, Daina Odonna herself came up on stage and stood beside the scowling daine.

"Child," she said, "you were off the music. That can happen to anyone the first time. Try once more."

Cerinthe ran back to the wings. As the melody played, she counted carefully and danced on stage again.

"Early!" Daine Rexall exclaimed. He turned toward the daina. "I told you she wouldn't…"

Daina Odonna held up one slender finger, and his mouth shut.

"Cerinthe," the daina said, "you can count music?"

Unable to speak, Cerinthe nodded and looked down at the floor, made of oak, like ships—like sinking ships. After what had happened this morning, she feared they would take both parts away. Daina Odonna came closer, her black skirt licking her black shoes with their diamond-shaped buckles. Cerinthe looked up. A thick layer of powder covered the daina's face, making white lines in the creases on her forehead.

"Congratulations," the daina said so softly that no one else could hear. "You didn't vomit."

"What?" asked Cerinthe, startled.

Daina Odonna smiled. "My first time on stage alone, not only did I miss my cue, I vomited!"

"You?"

"Me. Now stop trying so hard. Relax. Pretend that you're a princess frolicking in a beautiful palace. Try again, child."

Cerinthe walked back to the wings. The music began. One, two, three…she danced on cue. She knew the steps perfectly, but the feeling of being a princess eluded her. "Blowsy rose" kept echoing in her mind. Every watching eye seemed to burn through her tunic. Daina Odonna made her repeat the dance four times, stopping and starting her so often that she could scarcely remember where she was.

When her solo ended, Cerinthe did piqué turns off the stage as a screen rose behind her and revealed Sileree, who did piqué turns onto the stage. The younger princess and the older blended from one to the other without the dance ever stopping.

Cerinthe stood sweating in the wings. She knew she had danced poorly; there had been nothing in herself that she could reach. She didn't know how to "frolic." If the princess was as honey sweet as the choreography and music, she must be either very vain or a complete idiot.

"A good first attempt," Daina Lizabrina said, "though a bit stiff. You need more expression."

Cerinthe wiped her forehead, bewildered. As a rose she had too much expression, as the princess, not enough.

"Watch how Sileree does it," the daina added.

Cerinthe huddled closer to the curtain, wrapped her arms around her chest, and looked out at the stage.

Sileree's grimness vanished when she danced. Bright, vivacious, she lilted across the stage like a butterfly. Every movement, from the tilt of her head to the extension of her foot, suggested the graceful dignity of a princess. Cerinthe thought the choreography was better too. Perhaps Daine Rexall didn't know any children.

After dinner that night, Mistress Krissel made Cerinthe apologize to the girls for throwing the pie. She also placed Cerinthe on probation for one month.

"During that time," Mistress Krissel said, "you will receive no stipend." Every week, the school gave each student a small sum. "Also, any further violation of the rules will result in suspension." Cerinthe nodded, but she didn't care; she would do the same thing all over again.

Instead of going back to her room, Cerinthe wandered through the halls, up the side stairs, and down the back stairs until at last she found herself in the dispensary. She took the *Herbal* from the bookshelf and sat down at the table. Page fifty-two, page fifty-two clamored in her mind, but she ignored it. For the next half hour Cerinthe forgot her worries, engrossed in descriptions of lemon balm, verbena, and rosehips.

"Why, Cerinthe," said Sileree in the doorway.

Cerinthe blinked, still half in the world of root and seed and tincture. "Oh, hello."

"Is Mistress Blythe here?" Sileree asked hoarsely.

"No. Is your throat sore?"

"A little. With all the rehearsals lately, I think I'm worn

out." Sileree seemed sad and oddly still, nothing like the vivacious princess she had been on stage. "I hoped Mistress Blythe could do something for it."

Instantly, Cerinthe thought of a mixture of honey and lemon, with a measure of candoor…

"I simply can't get sick now," Sileree said. "Not with all the work for the ballet."

"I thought you danced beautifully. I wish I could dance just like you—be just like you someday."

"Don't!" Sileree turned rigid. A frantic look filled her eyes. "Don't be like me. Don't ever!"

Speechless, Cerinthe leaned back in her chair.

Sileree sagged against the shelves and rubbed her throat. "I'm sorry."

"That's all right," Cerinthe mumbled.

"It's…complicated. I'm too tired to explain. My throat feels…" Sileree grew sad and still again as if no breath or blood pulsed through her body.

Why shouldn't I be like you? Cerinthe wanted to ask. What's wrong?

"Are you sick too?" Sileree asked.

"Me? No. I'm just reading this *Herbal.*"

"Really?" Sileree took a step forward. "Do you know about healing? Can you help me?"

Cerinthe studied Sileree's tired eyes, her dull skin, her unnatural stillness. She had some sickness worse than a sore throat but nothing that seemed familiar. Suddenly, emblazoned across Cerinthe's mind was the word "Glimroot." Page fifty-two! GLIMROOT!

"No, I can't help you," Cerinthe said, shutting the book. "I'm sorry. I know nothing at all about…you see I'm only interested in plants."

Sileree nodded. "I'll go look for Mistress Blythe then." She turned to leave, then stopped. "Don't worry about what happened at the rehearsal. You're going to take on the role quite well; I can sense that. Daine Rexall is temperamental. Simply do what he says and ignore how you feel." And Sileree left.

Cerinthe sat staring after her, shaken to the root of her soul. Silence pressed against her back, against her shoulders and neck. She slumped down on the *Herbal* and felt the cold medallion press into her forehead.

Chapter Twenty

On Friday, Cerinthe received a letter from Old Skolla saying that he had arranged for Thordon to meet her at four o'clock on Saturday "beside Old Skolla's willow basket." Cerinthe's eyes sparkled. That's what she needed to feel like herself again, Thordon and the sea. But as her fingers smoothed and folded the rough brown paper into smaller and smaller squares, the sparkle faded. Leaving the school would be dangerous; she couldn't risk it while she was still on probation. She tucked the note in her pocket and went off to find Daina Lizabrina for another coaching session.

Saturday's rehearsal dragged on and on. Daine Rexall stormed across the stage, finding fault with everyone, even Daina Carroll and Sileree. His comments grew meaner and meaner, but Sileree only nodded and followed every direction, her face a blank mask. Cerinthe did the same when he shouted at her.

"You are dancing like a fishwife!" Daine Rexall clutched his curly hair. "Curve your hands! Make your body fluid!"

Cerinthe held back a scream and nodded politely. She didn't feel this, she didn't, she didn't. A brittle spot formed inside her like a crust around a wound. Finally, when she was dismissed at three o'clock, she knew she had to get away or she would explode.

And now here she was walking with Thordon along one of the piers on Majesty Bay, feeling better than she had in weeks. She shook off the heaviness from the rehearsal, stretched her arms over her head and looked across the water, which today rippled a plum-colored blue. On Normost, the sea never had such warm and vibrant hues.

"Standing inside a ship with the keel half built is like being inside the belly of a whale," Thordon was saying, "but with wooden ribs instead of bone." He laughed and stuck his hands in his pockets.

Cerinthe smiled at him. A mild, late-winter breeze blew his sandy hair into tufts. He was paler from working inside but otherwise looked exactly as he had on the *Morning Hope*. The same eager light glinted in his eyes.

"I'm glad your apprenticeship is going so well," Cerinthe said, pulling her hood forward. She wore her old brown cloak over her uniform; people would think it odd to see a little daina walking unattended with a young man. "But do you ever miss the Northern Reach?" she asked. "Or fishing?"

"I miss going out every day never knowing what I might catch. But learning something new is kind of like that. With shipbuilding, I go to work every day not knowing what I might learn. I like getting up in the morning." He rubbed the back of his neck and grinned. "Most mornings anyway. This one particularly."

Cerinthe pretended to look at a crate full of crabs; they thrust their claws through the slats, trying to escape.

"Then shipbuilding is the right work for you," she said, curling her right hand. What did she feel when she got out of bed in the morning? Her nails stabbed into her palm. One word throbbed in her mind. Dread. Her head went back, and her hood fell to her shoulders. Dread?

"In six more years I'll be a journeyman," Thordon said, "and then… Are you all right? You look strange."

"I'm fine. Guess I'm not used to fresh air anymore." She tried to laugh, but it sounded hollow. Thordon's hand brushed her elbow, hesitated, and then retreated behind his back. Embarrassed, Cerinthe hurried on. Their footsteps thumped on the creaking pier.

"Tell me about your school and your dancing," Thordon said at last.

"I don't know where to start," Cerinthe answered. Should she tell him about the terrible rehearsals or Tayla's banishment? Should she tell him about Elliana? Ask his advice about Sileree's outburst in the dispensary? Should she describe the *Herbal* and how she felt both drawn and repelled by it? And never could she tell him the Sea Maid had abandoned her; that wasn't the kind of thing people talked about, except to a priestess. Anything she said would sound dismal—dreadful.

"They gave me a part in a ballet for Princess Zandora's birthday," she said at last. That seemed safe.

"Hurray!" Thordon jumped in the air. A man with a coil of rope looped over one shoulder grinned at them. "That's better than a hold full of halibut," Thordon added. "What part are you going to dance?"

"I've two parts. In the first, I'm one of twelve roses."

"I can see you as a rose," Thordon said, looking intently at a sloop straining from its mooring lines. "Poor workmanship," he mumbled. "Timber full of shipworms too, I'll bet. What's the other part?"

"The young Princess Zandora."

"The princess?"

"It's a solo part. I'll be dancing before her and…her parents."

"Her parents!" Thordon stared at her. "You mean, the queen and king? You'll be dancing all alone on the stage in front of them?"

"And the rest of the audience too." Cerinthe's knees wobbled like jellyfish.

Thordon whistled, turned away, and stuffed his hands in his pockets. "I'd say you're doing pretty well then." His voice sounded distant. "They must think you're really good."

"It's hard though. I don't know how it feels to be a princess." She held up both hands. "I can't even seem to be the kind of rose they want. Everyone watches me all the time, criticizing every little move. It hurts."

"That's the price you pay, wanting to be up there with all those fancy folks."

Part of Cerinthe crumpled; she felt as a butterfly must, when it had dared spread its wings only to have them crushed. They passed three fishing boats without saying anything.

"I didn't mean to be complaining," she said.

"You weren't," he said but didn't look at her.

In front of the next boat, six shining fish—sea trotters the length of a man's leg—were lined up on the pier. The crew celebrated, slapping each other on the back. Cerinthe paused to admire the fish; sea trotters were rare in the Northern Reach.

"Our share will be good," said one fisherman to another. "We'll host a round in the alehouse tonight."

"Have you ever seen a finer catch, son?" another man called to Thordon. He winked toward Cerinthe. "Or a sweeter, juicer fish? Got to be a first-rate fisherman to land one like that."

Thordon scowled at the man, then walked on so fast that Cerinthe had to run to keep up.

"What's wrong?" she asked.

"Nothing. I just have to get back."

Cerinthe put one hand on her hip. "Well I can't be away much longer either. I'll get into terrible trouble if anyone finds out." She paused, and her hand fell. "It's been good to see you though."

He faced her, his grey eyes searching hers, and suddenly seemed very close. Cerinthe looked down, keeping her eyes on a piling that supported the pier. Pink anemones and bone-colored barnacles—clamped shut—covered the wood and stretched down into the water.

"I mean it's been good to see someone from the Northern Reach," she added quickly, then cursed herself.

"Oh. Right." Thordon turned away again.

Silently, they climbed a ramp back to Harbor Road.

Cerinthe glanced up at the southern end of the curving bay. Above the plum-colored water rose the green bluff of Healer's Hill. Above that, rose the sapphire sky. A glimmer of white shone through the dark, wind-bent firs on top of the hill. The mederi. Did they have more books like the *Herbal* up there?

Thordon walked straight ahead.

"Something's wrong," Cerinthe blurted. "I know it is. Why won't you tell me?"

Thordon stopped. "I—" and he looked out at the harbor. Two schooners sailed side by side out of Majesty Bay, rising and falling in unison on the waves. Then one pulled ahead, holding due south, while the other began a slow, graceful tack to the east.

"When I've finished my apprenticeship," Thordon said, "I intend to journey to the New Western Isles."

"Thordon!"

A year ago, explorers had discovered a chain of uninhabited islands far to the west. Queen Seaborne had asked Nemaree for their care-taking in the name of Windward. Only three voyages had been made so far.

"Why do you want to go there?" Cerinthe asked. "Isn't the Northern Reach far enough away from the rest of the world?"

"The Isles are waiting to be explored. Who knows what's there? Or what's beyond?" Thordon slammed his right fist into his left palm. "It's a place to begin over. To make something new, to do things right. They'll need men like me. I plan to start my own shipyard one day. Then I'll be master and tell other men what to do."

Cerinthe thought of Daine Rexall shouting orders. A

moment later she said, "But traveling to the Isles—that doesn't explain why you got so upset."

Thordon hesitated; he plucked the frayed edge of his pocket. "The truth is, I'm worried about you."

"Me?"

"Now that you've got this big part, you have to be careful. Don't get used to a grand life, because you won't always be able to live like that."

"What do you mean?"

"Well you're not going to dance forever. Once you're old enough to get married, you'll quit. You're a commoner; you'll have to settle for a common man."

"Quit?" Cerinthe stared at him. "Have you any idea how hard dancing is? Or how sore my muscles get? I didn't sail three hundred leagues just to mark time. Dancing is my dream."

"But you'll want to have children. Make a home for…your husband."

"Not if I have to stop dancing. Will you stop building ships once you marry?"

"That's different…" he began as a carriage slowed beside them.

"Why, good afternoon!" called a voice.

Cerinthe saw purple, then the flash of spinning golden spirals. Framed in the carriage window, leaning languidly on her elbows, was Elliana. Her chin rested in her hands. The frothy lace on her sleeves had slid back, exposing her white forearms. Her red curls, pinned up loosely, half-tumbled down one side of her face. She smiled her most dazzling smile at Thordon.

"How wonderful to see you here, Cerinthe," she called, waving as the carriage rolled past.

"What a beauty," Thordon said. "Who is she?"

Cerinthe stood frozen. "Elliana. From the school. She's sure to tell that I've been out—and with a boy. I'm in terrible trouble. I have to get back!" Cerinthe began to run.

"Can I do anything?" Thordon called.

"No!" she shouted over her shoulder. "Yes! They may expel me. I'll need a job!" She saw him smile.

Dread, Cerinthe thought as she ran. Dread.

Chapter Twenty-one

When Cerinthe arrived back at the school, no one was waiting for her. No one seemed to have missed her. For the rest of the evening she paced her room, waiting for a summons from Daina Odonna until finally Isalette said, "For the sea's sake, go somewhere else!" So Cerinthe went to the dispensary and tried to read the *Herbal,* but she kept staring at the scale on the mahogany counter instead.

She knew that she had risked everything—her dream of being a dancer, her future, even the roof over her head—by her two visits to Majesty Bay. And yet, she felt as though she would have died if she hadn't made them.

Cerinthe shut the *Herbal.* Before she was expelled, she needed to find some way to say goodbye to Tayla. But how? Cerinthe tugged her collar and looked at the empty table where the scallop bowl had stood. She remembered the first time she had been in this room. Her eyes lit up.

"That's it!" she exclaimed.

Later that night, after the bell struck two, Cerinthe opened the door to the laundry. She listened. Silence. She glanced over her shoulder down the dark hallway. Nothing. This time no one had followed her. She stepped in and shut the door. When she uncovered her candle, the mounds of laundry loomed up like giants in the flickering light. Cerinthe tiptoed past, as though afraid she might waken them.

In the folding room, she searched the shelves until she found a smudge's uniform, which she pulled on over her nightgown. On one of the bottom shelves, she found a long row of quilts piled six high. She made a nest behind them, curled up, and blew out the candle.

The room turned utterly black. Wide-awake, Cerinthe blinked into the darkness. Why hadn't she received a summons yet? Was Elliana simply waiting until morning to reveal what she had seen? Cerinthe wedged her knees against the wall. Would Daina Odonna expel her immediately or wait until after *Archipelago Princess*? And what would she do? Where would she go?

She had saved money from her weekly stipend but not enough for passage home. Besides, she didn't want to go home. Could she find another job in Faranor? If she was lucky, she might be a smudge somewhere else; she had no other skills.

Cerinthe pointed one toe under the quilts. Was her dream of being a dancer over forever?

Then, as she often did at night, Cerinthe closed her eyes

and imagined Thordon's arms around her, but now it brought no comfort. Why had he become so cold when he learned she had been given the role of the Princess? How did that affect his plans to settle in the New Western Isles? What made him think she would stop dancing when she was old enough to marry? If only Elliana hadn't interrupted them. Cerinthe spun into sleep like a rock into a whirlpool, a whirlpool showing Thordon's face over and over, Thordon's face looking at Elliana as though she were the most divinely beautiful young woman he had ever seen....

The sound of muffled voices and thumping feet woke her. Cerinthe yawned, still tired. The windowless room was as black as ever. Because the servants rose two hours before the students, no one above stairs would miss her. Cerinthe folded the quilts. After stuffing her hair into the grey cap and pulling it down to her eyebrows, she went to the door, cracked it open, and waited.

Doors banged. Water pumps hissed. The smudges filed in for another day in the damp dungeon. As soon as ten of them were milling around, Cerinthe slipped in. She knew that Mistress Dalyrimple would linger over breakfast for another twenty minutes. Keeping her head down, Cerinthe crossed the sorting room and entered the washroom.

The smell hit her first: the acrid mixture of dirty clothes, yellow laundry soap, and wet stone—a smell she would never forget. Already, steam hovered in the air. Cerinthe waded from tub to tub, looking for Tayla. In their grey uniforms, the smudges all looked the same, differing only by height or weight.

Someone coughed a long, racking cough. Cerinthe turned.

There, in the dampest corner of the room, doubled over a tub, was Tayla. Her thin shoulder blades poked against the back of her grey uniform. When Cerinthe sidled up to the tub, Tayla didn't bother to look up. Her curls straggled against her forehead.

"Tayla," Cerinthe whispered. "Don't make a move or show any surprise. It's me, Cerinthe."

Tayla's hands stopped scrubbing. Then she sniffed loudly, took her hands from the water, shook them, dried them on her apron, and fished for her handkerchief. As she blew her nose, she glanced at Cerinthe's face. Her eyes widened.

"I haven't much time," Cerinthe whispered. "I'm so sorry, Tayla. It's all my fault this happened to you."

Tayla stuffed her handkerchief in her pocket and glanced around. "I could use some help with this cloak here," she said loudly. "It's terrible heavy."

Cerinthe rolled up her sleeves and plunged her hands into the tub. "I'm probably going to be expelled," she whispered.

"Expelled, Miss!"

"Shh! I came to say good-bye."

Tayla coughed again.

"That sounds bad," Cerinthe said.

"Just a cold." Tayla shrugged. "Like everybody else in here's got. I'm awful glad to see you. I was afraid you thought I broke your Mama's seagull, and it's about broke my heart to think you did."

"Never! Elliana did it. I've been trying for weeks to get down to see you, but I always got caught. Listen. I've got to go before Dalyrimple comes." Cerinthe felt tears in her eyes.

"Good-bye, Tayla. Fair winds be yours."

"Oh, don't go away without me!" Tayla pleaded. "Take me with you. I've got some wages saved."

"But I don't know where I'm going, or what I'm going to do. We might end up beggars."

Tayla shook her head so hard that her cap tipped over her left ear. "I don't care. If you get expelled, take me with you. Anything's better than this. Please."

Cerinthe looked at Tayla's peaked face and nodded. "I'll think of something, I promise. They may turn me out today, but I hope they wait until after *Archipelago Princess*. Then I'll have time to make a plan. Be ready for anything the next time you see me."

"It'll give me something good to think of," Tayla said. She coughed again. Cerinthe squeezed her hand under the water and slogged out of the washroom.

The rest of that day, Cerinthe waited in dread, but hour after agonizing hour passed and the summons never came. Another day went by and another, and still nothing happened. Elliana occasionally gazed over Cerinthe's head with a secretive smile but most of the time simply ignored her.

On Wednesday, the Sea Maid's Festival began. As the students walked through the city on their way to the temple, Cerinthe wished Elliana would simply tell and get it over with. What was she waiting for? The students crossed a road crowded with celebrating people who threw handfuls of crushed scallop shells. The fragments clung to Cerinthe's hair and crunched beneath her shoes. A lady rode slowly past; the white plume on her hat stirred delicately, like a hand fluttering over a yawn. Three ragged girls ran after her, shouting, fighting each other to be in front.

"Polish your boots, Lady! A shellnar a boot."

"Don't trust their shoddy work. Mine's the best shine in Faranor!"

"They's robbers. Two boots for a shellnar! Spit's free!"

Cerinthe looked away. She, too, might be that desperate soon. In front of an alehouse, a troop of street dancers spun in scarlet costumes that flashed with bangles and sequins. When they saw the students in their blue cloaks, they stopped dancing and watched them pass. Elliana waved to a dancer who wore a shiny emerald sash. She waved back and did a quick entrechat—a jump into the air with a quick beat of the feet—a rather good entrechat, Cerinthe noticed. Would they let her join their troop if she was expelled?

The students turned a corner, and Cerinthe stopped abruptly. Before her rose the Temple of the Sea Maid, fashioned of cream-colored stone faintly shimmering, like sunlight on sand. Cerinthe tried to forget Elliana, forget the other girls, forget that she felt like a herded goat, and concentrate instead on the Goddess. *Sea Maid*, Cerinthe prayed. *On this day celebrating Your birth, let me hear You sing again.*

A winding route led into the temple, its curving marble slabs etched with spirals, fish, and triple serpents. When Cerinthe reached the outer sanctum, her mouth opened. The wooden temple on Normost had not prepared her for such magnificence.

Carved in white-veined aquamarine marble, the Sea Maid's face covered a wall two stories high and twice as long. Her hair rippled out like waves or snakes or cirrus clouds, stretching from wall to wall as though encompassing the entire world. Swathes of delicate netting—sacred netting that must never touch the ground—festooned the carving. Shiny and phosphorescent, they imitated the foam that sheathed the Sea Maid when she was born.

"Fruitful be the sea foam," an acolyte said to each person.

Cerinthe followed the others and sat on one of the stone risers that angled up from the temple floor. She looked down at the altar, a perfect scallop shell some six feet long. The upper half stood open like a lid on a treasure chest. In the bottom half were bouquets of tulips and roses, bottles of wine, bolts of blue silk, and baskets of asparagus and oranges—all intertwined with gleaming strands of pearls. One person at a time knelt before the scallop shell and offered a gift.

"Pray," another acolyte told Cerinthe and those around her. "Then join the line to the altar."

Cerinthe gazed at the vast carved face. *Sea Maid, Bringer of the Dawn, my offering is a poem about the dance I made to honor Your birth.* She fingered a tiny scroll of paper in her pocket. *I tried to explain what the dance means to me, how much I want You to come back. Please accept it. Fill me with Your presence when I perform it for Daine Miekel's class—and when I dance the princess part too. And one more thing. Help Thordon to understand how important dancing is to me.* Cerinthe kept praying but sensed nothing. Finally, after all the other students had joined the line, she sighed and followed them. A young man in front of her clutched a white swan, a bird sacred to the Sea Maid.

When Elliana reached the head of the line, she spoke to the high priestess who had visited on the Day of the Dark Moon. The priestess listened, then led Elliana behind a screen on the right. The line stopped moving.

"What's happening?" the young man whispered.

"Shh!" Cerinthe shook her head.

Everyone waited. On a wooden table in front of the screen, the acolytes struck mallets against an array of glass vessels, each containing a different amount of water. Silvery tones trembled through the air. A child rubbed a metal drum, making a low continuous note like the roar of the sea.

At last the priestess returned, looking delighted. "My children," she said, "I ask you all to kneel."

Elliana stepped out from behind the screen: her feet bare, her hair loose. In the center of the sanctuary, she flung off her cloak and stood naked. A murmur ran through the temple. Cerinthe shut her eyes, counted to four, and then opened them again. Not only was Elliana still naked, now she was crouched on the floor with one leg bent and the other pointing toward the altar. Cerinthe stiffened. A priestess began to sing, her clear soprano voice soaring into *The Aria of the Sea Maid.*

Elliana's fingers fluttered. Her wrist lifted, fell again, and then her arm swept up to greet the sky. Still crouched, she rocked with the swell of the waves. It was *The Dance of the Sea Maid,* and Elliana danced it more divinely than ever before. The Sea Maid Herself seemed to be sailing on Her scallop shell before them.

No! Cerinthe wanted to cry. Stop! She had prayed for the

Sea Maid's presence, and here it was before her, though not as she had envisioned. *Through me*, Cerinthe prayed. *Through me, not her. She's a thief and a liar! It isn't fair. She's stealing my gift to You.* But for the next few minutes, Cerinthe could only sit and watch, crumpling the scroll in her pocket. Now she knew why no summons had come from Daina Odonna: Elliana was claiming the Sea Maid's dance as her own. It was blackmail—the price for Elliana's silence about the incident on Harbor Road.

No wonder the priestess had looked delighted. What better gift to offer at the Sea Maid's Festival than a dance depicting Her sacred birth? Even if Cerinthe had thought of performing the dance here, she would never have dared—and never in the nude. Yet, she saw now that this was exactly how the dance was meant to be performed. Elliana radiated the divine energy of the holy body of woman. However, by dancing naked in the temple, something only priestesses did, Elliana was offering herself as an acolyte. What had made her change her mind about joining the temple?

Beside Cerinthe, the young man with the white swan stared at Elliana with his mouth open. He stroked the swan faster and faster.

As Cerinthe crushed the paper between her thumb and forefinger, a sense of shock seeped through her anger. Elliana had broken the oath she'd sworn in Kasakol's name. Cerinthe believed her capable of anything except that. What had she said exactly? "I wouldn't dance your stupid dance in front of Daine Miekel for all the gold in Windward." To be precise, Elliana hadn't broken the oath: Daine Miekel was not here.

The singer's voice streamed in a bright arpeggio. Elliana changed the choreography and spun in a series of chaîné turns along the edge of the carved wall. Her hair whipped round, brushing the wall over and over until a length of the sacred shiny net caught on her curls. With a quick arabesque, she resumed Cerinthe's choreography. Cerinthe could not look away. Would the net fall? Did Elliana know it was there? She leaped into a grand jeté and the net streamed out like a comet's tail. At the crest of the jump, it flew free, darted in little dips and dives, and then fell in a glimmering heap on the floor.

All over the temple, people gasped.

"Ah!" The young man dropped the white swan, which padded away. The delight on the priestess's face changed to horror.

When Elliana reached the place in the dance where she had stopped working with Cerinthe, she ended the dance abruptly. Cerinthe sat stunned while the singer finished the aria. Elliana seemed surprised that no one was watching her. She turned in the direction the priestess was staring, then dropped like an anchor and lay face down, prostrate on the floor.

Cerinthe frowned. Elliana had reacted too quickly, too dramatically. Anyone else would have frozen in shock, at least for a moment. In a flash, Cerinthe understood; this was all another of Elliana's schemes. The priestess could never make her an acolyte now. And because she had danced naked in public, no nobleman—even Lord Mardlehop—would have Elliana for his wife. In one brilliant, sacrilegious stroke, she had solved her two biggest problems. At what price, though? The high priestess could kill her.

"Oh no!" the young man whispered, gulping. The white swan had wandered out onto the temple floor.

The high priestess walked over to the netting, which fluttered when she picked it up, showing a long rip down the middle. Over and over she pulled the torn edges together, but each time the rip fell open again. At last the priestess looked up, as if remembering where she was.

Her face angry, she strode over to Elliana, whose white body still pressed against the blue marble floor. The other priestesses closed around Elliana and the high priestess until they were blocked from sight. In the middle of the circle, a knife was raised, its blade shining. Cerinthe sagged against the young man, who sagged against her.

At that moment, the white swan honked. He waddled over to the edge of the circle, where he arched up and flapped his wings. The circle opened. The high priestess stared at him, hesitating, the knife in her hand. He honked again.

"Acla, Nemaree!" the priestess cried in the holy language. As she bowed her head, the circled closed again. The knife fell. There was no cry, no sound except for the breathing of the people in the temple. Then, while the high priestess bore the net away, the other priestesses returned to their places, leaving Elliana alone on the floor.

Cut into her back were three vertical red lines crossed by three horizontal ones: the stigma of the net defiler. She would bear forever the scar of this day, but she would live. The white swan settled on her feet and began to preen beneath one wing.

Cerinthe straightened. She should have guessed the high priestess would be lenient—doubtless Elliana had guessed it too. The priestess would believe that Elliana had been trying to honor the Sea Maid and would never dream the desecration had been deliberate.

Deliberate. Cerinthe pressed her knees together to stop them from shaking. No one could ever perform her dance now. Her gift had been wrenched from her, used to desecrate the very Goddess it had been made to honor. And yet, in spite of Elliana's sacrilege, the Sea Maid had helped her again, sent the white swan that may have saved her life.

The procession resumed. When Cerinthe's turn came, she knelt before the altar and shuffled the paper pebbles in the bottom of her pocket—the remnants of her poem. She felt cold as a stone, empty, lost in an angry black sea. It didn't hurt. She didn't feel it; she didn't. But tiny cracks splintered the stone until her body began to ache from her ankles to her throat. Cerinthe looked at the prostrate girl who had stolen a piece of her soul, and then looked back at the altar. She had no offering, no offering but hate.

Chapter Twenty-two

Throughout the two weeks that followed, each time Cerinthe opened her mouth she feared a scream might come out. She walked and danced with her jaw clenched. She went to bed with her knees pulled to her chin. Each night, she dreamed she was swimming underwater, seeking some lost, bright object among the orange starfish clinging to the rocks. Deeper she dove, down past the oysters that would not surrender their secrets, and deeper yet, until she grew terrified of the void beneath and kicked back toward the surface.

Night after night, she woke before dawn, exhausted but unable to sleep again. The instant she woke, she remembered how Elliana had desecrated the dance; how Tayla's curls had drooped, her thin shoulders shaking from the cough; how Thordon had not written; and how the Sea Maid continued

Her silence. Then tension squeezed her body so strongly that Cerinthe feared she might have some illness.

An elbow-shaped crack sprawled on the ceiling over her bed. As the dawn came, she would watch the crack gradually appear and would try to think, though her mind felt muddled. Even though she hadn't been expelled, Cerinthe was determined to find a way to help Tayla.

When the morning bell clanged on Tuesday, Cerinthe pulled her eyes away from the crack and dragged herself out of bed. Where would she find the strength for another long day of rehearsal?

With the performance of *Archipelago Princess* only ten days away, the Royal Theatre was in chaos. Scenery painters splashed daubs of pink, pale green, and gold on the backdrops and screens. Carpenters hammered. Stagehands cursed over their pulleys and lanterns. The seamstresses, looking like anemones with all the pin cushions bristling on their wrists, chased the dancers everywhere.

Backstage, behind a half-finished bower of silk roses, Cerinthe began to stretch. Lutes, horns, harps, and drums piped and trilled and boomed as the musicians warmed up in the pit between the stage and seats. Soon the cacophony stopped, and the rehearsal began. When Scene One had nearly ended, Daina Lizabrina nodded to Cerinthe. Wide awake now, she ran to the wings.

One, two, three…Cerinthe danced onto the stage, holding out her skirt. Four chassés, the piqués, then the fouettés—six, seven, eight—and on until she was one minute into her two-minute solo.

"Cease!" Daina Odonna exclaimed. A viol crooned one last note that slid into a short shriek as the bow lifted, and the musicians, rustling and rattling, put their instruments down.

Cerinthe stopped and blinked into the stage lights. What now? She shaded her eyes, looked out into the dark audience, and saw Daina Odonna standing on the other side of the orchestra pit.

"Come to the edge of the stage," the daina said. "At once."

Cerinthe ran forward. Daina Odonna's powdered white face gleamed oddly, lit up from beneath by the musicians' lanterns. The yellow light brushed her throat, the tips of her nostrils, and then the hollow between her eyes and brows.

She studied Cerinthe silently. Over a hundred people—the artisans and apprentices; the dancers, staff, and servants involved in such a massive ballet—watched from the audience. They included, Cerinthe knew, the first rose of the Rose Court: Elliana. Cerinthe could feel all the eyes crawling over her from the darkness. Why didn't the daina speak? Cerinthe clenched one hand and scraped her nails against her palm.

"Do you realize, child," Daina Odonna's voice filled the theatre, "that there are only ten more days until the performance?"

"Were...the fouettés wrong?" Cerinthe asked.

"It is not a question of the fouettés!" The daina threw out her arm and snapped her fingers. "You dance without expression. Is there no feeling in your heart? You are a princess, a rich little girl. Your parents are the queen and king. One day, you yourself will be Queen of Windward. But now, today, you are ten years old: gay, light, like a little flower. You must do more than dance the steps. You must feel the part."

"Yes, Daina." Cerinthe wiggled her big toe against the hole in her slipper. Daina Odonna had made this speech before, and Cerinthe had tried and tried to please her but simply didn't know how.

"Technically, you are a skilled dancer for your age, child," the daina said. "I think this must be a failure of the imagination, even…" she held up her hands "…a failure of the soul itself."

Cerinthe reeled backward as though she'd been slapped. The stage lights blurred. A failure of the *soul*? Could that be true? Could that be why the Sea Maid no longer sang to her? She saw herself kneeling before the scallop altar, her big hands empty.

"A dancer is an artist," Daina Odonna said, clasping the ruby on her breast. "She must have passion burning in her heart. Passion burning so brightly that the audience, too, can feel it. Have you no passion, child?"

Cerinthe fought to keep her chin from trembling. Tears filled her eyes.

Daina Odonna sighed. "Perhaps we should approach this another way. Tell me, when have you been the happiest in your life? The most alive—the most full of joy?"

"When I learned I'd been accepted by the school."

"No!" Daina Odonna banged the railing.

Cerinthe jumped.

"Listen! I refer to your life before you came here. Think, Cerinthe. Where would you go this moment, if you could, to get away from here?" The daina leaned forward. "To get away from me?"

Cerinthe stared at the yellow-white face that appeared almost disembodied against the dark theatre. She closed her eyes. A wave of longing swept over her, a wave so powerful it nearly knocked her to her knees.

Her mind filled with a picture of the herb garden behind the cottage on Normost. She saw her hands in the dirt, transplanting a rosemary seedling, then pulling a weed. She saw the earthenware jars in Gwimma's dispensary, and smelled rose-bay, delicate and woodsy, drying overhead. She saw her hands again, this time sewing up yet another cut in young Donney Beech's knee. Outside, the ball of the sun was being drunk by the ocean at sunset, sizzling violet and red and gold. She reached toward the horizon where blue met blue as she danced on the beach to the sound of the Sea Maid singing on the northwest wind....

"Yes," Daina Odonna said softly. "Yes! I can see that you are feeling something. Now, tell me where you were happiest."

"In the garden and the dispensary." Cerinthe could scarcely speak. "On the beach too." And, she thought, when the Sea Maid sang.

"I cannot hear you," said the daina.

Cerinthe became aware of all the people listening and said only, "I was happiest on the beach at Normost."

"Then think of that when you dance the part."

"But it has nothing to do with being a princess," Cerinthe said. Besides, that was the most private part of herself. How could she show it to everyone?

"Well, it's the best we can do," the daina said. "Now try once more. Let your heart fill with thoughts of your beach."

The music started again. Cerinthe danced. She thought of the garden and Gwimma's dispensary. She smelled the herbs, heard the sea and the wind. Near the bluff, her mother and father rowed side by side in the skiff. Cerinthe danced on the beach, her heart so filled with home that for a moment she thought she was home. Then, with a sharp clap the picture vanished, and she was trembling on the stage in the Royal Theatre.

"Now you've forgotten the steps!" Daina Odonna exclaimed.

Cerinthe took a deep breath. The steps, those silly, pretentious steps of the young princess! She had changed them without even thinking. They had nothing to do with home.

Daina Odonna crossed her arms. The arrow-sharp points of her black sleeves seemed etched on her white hands. The ruby sparkled darkly.

"We are going to do this again and again until you perform as I tell you," she said. "Now, I saw true feeling that time. Go back and put it into the proper choreography. Work."

Cerinthe put her hands on her hips and scowled. All the confusion, pain, sorrow, and anger that had built up inside her came bursting out.

"That doesn't make any sense!" she blurted. "The choreography doesn't match the feeling. How can I put passion into such silly steps?"

The entire theatre grew suddenly silent, gaping like an enormous black cavern. Daina Odonna's look of patient forbearance changed to ice.

"How dare you?" she said. "Daine Rexall," she called over her shoulder. He stepped forward.

"I told you," he said. "I knew all along she wouldn't do."

"Cerinthe," the daina said. "Daine Rexall has choreographed ten—is it ten, Rexall, am I correct?"

"Twelve, actually," he said, sliding his jaw to the right.

"Twelve dances in the company's repertoire. He knows Princess Zandora personally. Are you suggesting that this man, with all his experience and knowledge, does not know what he is doing? And that you, a mere child, do?"

Cerinthe looked down at Daine Rexall, who looked coldly back. She remembered how he had threatened to take away the part of the rose "for her own good." The daine and daina stood together, an impenetrable fortress, their faces almost cadaverous in the yellow light.

Cerinthe's hands fell to her sides. "No, no of course not. That's not what I meant," she said miserably. "I'm sorry."

"Then do as you are told," Daina Odonna said. "If you continue to talk back to your betters and make excuses, I assure you, you will never be a daina in my company."

Sobbing now, Cerinthe ran back to the wings. The musicians began to play the sweet, mincing melody, and Cerinthe danced Daine Rexall's silly steps with tears falling down her cheeks.

Chapter Twenty-three

Back in the theatre dressing room, Cerinthe pulled on her uniform; the broadcloth felt stiff and unyielding. Her head ached. Girls chattered around her, splashing in basins of water, unwinding gauze from their toes, and rubbing ointment into sore muscles. Everyone ignored her, whether out of sympathy or derision she didn't know.

Elliana's voice drifted through the alcove that separated the dressing room from the hall. "This ballet will be a disaster because of her. We shall all be humiliated before the queen and—"

"Be quiet!" someone warned. "She'll hear you." Their voices faded as they walked away.

In the sudden silence, Cerinthe reached behind her neck and fastened the top buttons on her dress, hiding her face in the crook of her elbow.

"Elliana's a fine one to talk about humiliating us," Sileree said as she pulled out strands of hair caught in her diamond comb. "After what she did in the temple."

"You have to admit the choreography was brilliant," Juna said. "The teachers are still buzzing about it. For a moment there, I thought the little vixen really was the Goddess."

Cerinthe yanked a button so hard that it came off in her bandaged hand. She had scratched her palm until it bled. The first day she had worn this uniform, Tayla had buttoned it. That seemed like a lifetime ago. When had her dream become a nightmare?

The daina's terrible words battered Cerinthe's mind: a failure of the imagination, a failure of the soul. If she had no soul, why did her heart hurt so much? If only she could have pointed to *The Dance of the Sea Maid* and said, "Look! I have imagination. See? I have passion and a soul...."

Cerinthe left the last button undone, grabbed her bag, and fled. Halfway down the hall, she turned and walked back because she had left her dancing slippers on the bench.

"And I say Daina Odonna shouldn't have been so hard on her!" exclaimed a familiar voice, Sileree's voice.

Cerinthe stopped, unseen, in the alcove outside the dressing room.

"She's a child!" Sileree added. "She's only been in the school for a few months."

"So?" Juna said. "Admit it. You're partial to her because she adores you like a puppy."

"That's beside the point. Daina Odonna shouldn't have

mortified her in front of everyone."

Juna snorted. "You know very well that she did it on purpose, to stir Cerinthe up, to pull some emotion out of her."

"There's a difference between criticism and humiliation. The daina was cruel."

"I've taken worse—and so have you. The sooner Cerinthe learns that a dancer's life is difficult, the better off she'll be." Juna clicked her tongue. "Pity the daina gave Cerinthe the part. 'Her Highness' would have made a perfect princess. Too bad Daina Odonna felt she had to teach Elliana a lesson."

Cerinthe pressed her knuckles against her mouth.

"But I thought Cerinthe got the part because Elliana's too tall?" someone asked.

"No," said another voice, "because she has Sileree's coloring."

"Those were all reasons," Juna said, "but Elliana's laziness was the big one. The daina hoped to shame her into working harder. Waste of time, if you ask me. Maybe she'll become a choreographer."

Cerinthe felt as if she were drowning; her lungs inhaled water; her eyes stared and saw nothing, no bubbles, no blackness. Was it true? Had the daina chosen her only to teach Elliana a lesson? Cerinthe backed away from the dressing room. But what did that have to do with her? With the person she was inside? Nothing! She ran down to the stage door and stumbled, sobbing, out into the courtyard.

The tall, crystalline towers of Faranor loomed above her, cold and stern, as sharp as pins, unreachable. Footsteps came running behind her.

"Wait," called Sileree.

Cerinthe walked faster.

Sileree ran up and held out Cerinthe's dancing slippers. "You forgot these."

"Oh," Cerinthe mumbled. "Thanks."

"If you like, I'll walk back with you," Sileree said softly. The skin beneath her eyes looked bruised.

Cerinthe nodded. As they crossed the courtyard, a bleak spring wind ruffled the grass struggling to grow between the paving stones.

"I know the daina was mean," Sileree said at last, "but she thought it was for your own good. To make you a better dancer."

"How does being mean make me better?"

"It doesn't make *you* better; it makes you a better *dancer.*" Sileree sighed. "Understand. Daina Odonna believes dancing is the only thing under sea or sky."

"But it is."

"Not for me."

Startled, Cerinthe stopped and looked at her. A still, tight expression spread over her face, the same expression Cerinthe had seen in the dispensary.

"How can you say that?" Cerinthe asked. "You're one of the best dancers in the school."

"That shows you how wrong the daina is, doesn't it?"

"I don't understand."

Sileree walked on. "I don't care about dancing with every drop of blood in my veins. Because I have to dance, I want to be good, that's all. If great passion and imagination were essential, as the daina insists, would I be one of the best dancers in the school?"

"I…I don't know."

"Some people do care that much—Juna does. But just wanting and working for something passionately is no guarantee of success, even if you have talent."

They reached the fountain. The bronze sculpture of the dancers looked blurred, the identical bodies frozen, captured in some mockery of time.

Cerinthe said, "But the teachers say if you work hard enough—"

"I know. Work hard enough, sacrifice everything, keep dancing even if you're sick or injured and you'll be the greatest dancer in the kingdom! Another Kasakol!" Sileree swung her bag toward the fountain and hit the stone with a thud. "Lies!"

Cerinthe stepped back.

"I've seen talented students here who worked themselves to the bone," Sileree said. "They did everything they were told and more, and still didn't succeed. Then their failure's blamed on some supposed lack in them: They didn't really try hard enough, or want it enough, or they didn't have enough passion or character."

Sileree threw back her shoulders. "Why don't the teachers teach the truth? Sometimes things don't work out, and it's nobody's fault."

Cerinthe wet her lips. "But if you don't love dancing, why did you become a dancer?"

"It wasn't my idea." Sileree's lovely voice flattened. "It wasn't what I wanted to be."

"What did you want to be?"

"An opera singer."

"Then why?..."

Sileree swung her bag again, bumping the stone over and over until the strap twisted around her arm.

"My aunt and uncle are poor," she said. "They lost all their money in my parents' shipping line. Six ships sank in a year—my parents on one of them. Aunt and Uncle raised me even though they had six younger children. When I was ten, they sent me here."

"Why not to a singing school?" Cerinthe asked.

"None of them are free. Uncle thought if I became a daina, I could provide for them—and educate and dower my cousins too." The strap wound tighter and tighter until it squeezed Sileree's arm. "And now I've been offered a place in the royal company when I graduate."

"That's wonderful!"

"It's too late to start all over again," Sileree continued as if she hadn't heard. "I owe them everything. I have no other way to earn the kind of living they deserve." Her eyes darkened and her face crumpled.

"I have become what someone else wanted me to be!" she cried. "And now I'm trapped. Oh Nemaree! I'm trapped...." She tore off the strap, then dropped her bag and ran.

"Wait!" Cerinthe called, but Sileree skirted the fountain and raced across the courtyard, disappearing into the crowded street beyond.

Cerinthe clutched her dancing slippers to her chest. How could this be? Sileree was everything Cerinthe had dreamed of being, yet she was desperately unhappy. "Don't be like me,"

Sileree had said in the dispensary. "Don't ever!" Cerinthe took three steps after her, then stopped, staring at the clogged jets sputtering in the fountain. Her bones felt as heavy as the marble steps leading up to the school. All she wanted to do was crawl into bed and collapse.

She left Sileree's bag with the doorman. When he bowed, Cerinthe longed to pop his puffed purple sleeves with a pin. Next, she dragged herself to the mailroom, but Thordon still had not written. At last Cerinthe reached the pearls' wing and pressed the latch on her bedroom door, only to see Mistress Blythe come bustling down the hall.

"There you are," Mistress Blythe called, "thank goodness."

Cerinthe groaned inside; she didn't want to talk to anyone.

"Tayla is terribly sick," Mistress Blythe said.

"What?" Cerinthe dropped the latch; it clattered. "Tayla? Sick?"

"I'm afraid so. I warned Mistress Odue that Tayla's constitution was too delicate for the laundry. She caught a cold, and with all the dreadful damp down there, it's settled in her chest." Mistress Blythe plucked at her bodice. "I know it's against the rules for students to mix with servants, but she's been asking for you. And Mistress Krissel has given permission. Will you come?"

"Of course." Cerinthe followed Mistress Blythe down to the dispensary and into one of the sick rooms where Tayla lay in bed.

"Miss Cerinthe!" she said hoarsely.

"Hello, Tayla." Cerinthe forced her voice to sound cheerful. "I'm sorry you're sick."

"I almost don't mind—it's so nice having a window to look

out." Tayla tried to smile but coughed instead.

Cerinthe remembered the dark, close room where the laundry maids slept. She knew how dismal it was. Oh, why hadn't she thought of a way to get Tayla out of there? Tayla's face was red, her eyes bright. Cerinthe didn't need to touch her to know she had a fever and probably pneumonia.

"I'll go mix up some more medicine for you, Tayla dear," Mistress Blythe said, "while you and Cerinthe have a nice visit."

"Tayla," Cerinthe whispered. "I didn't get expelled. I was trying to think of a way to get you out of the dungeon anyway…and then with *The Dance of the Sea*…I mean with the ballet just days away and everything so awful…" Cerinthe's voice broke. "I couldn't think of a way. I should have thought harder. I should have run away with you anyway! I'm sorry."

"It's all right, Miss. I'm out now, aren't I?" Tayla raised her head off her pillow. "You tried, I know you did. Don't you go blaming yourself none; it'll just make me feel worse."

"But—"

"Tell me about the costumes for the ballet. Oh, are they lovely? Come on, do."

So Cerinthe described in infinite detail the tulle and ribbons and lace while Tayla's smile grew bigger and bigger. In the midst of a debate over the incredible number of costume pearls sewn on the queen's dress, Tayla began coughing again; she expelled brackish phlegm into a basin. After Tayla fell asleep, Cerinthe tiptoed back into the dispensary's main room and looked at the medicine Mistress Blythe was stirring.

"A little honey, hot water, and whiskey to soothe her poor

throat," Mistress Blythe said.

"But," Cerinthe began, then stopped. Gwimma's pneumonia remedies called for stronger measures. Tayla needed a mustard plaster and a decoction of the root of tarwood for the putrid phlegm, and she shouldn't be lying flat on her back, and the window should be open. Cerinthe glanced at *Leigh's Herbal* on the shelf. According to the *Herbal*, Gwimma had used giress in a way that could be fatal. What if she was wrong about her pneumonia remedies too?

Tayla began coughing again. Cerinthe stood, torn. The urge to help was like a wind pushing her forward, but the memory of the Black Ship pulled her back. No, she wouldn't risk hurting someone ever again. She was not a healer, and, according to Daina Odonna, she was not a dancer either. She was nothing but a person with a failed soul.

Steam trailed from the hot, useless, honey drink and disappeared into the air.

Cerinthe wanted to scream. Life was not supposed to be filled with wicked girls who hurt innocent maids, with mothers who died and left their children, or with teachers who demeaned their students. There should be no beggars, Black Ships, and deadly herbs. No dreams that twisted into nightmares or sputtered into mists where they vanished altogether. Cerinthe glared at the corner table where the scallop bowl had stood. Nor was the Goddess supposed to abandon you when you needed Her most, abandon you and help a lying, sacrilegious thief!

Sea Maid, Cerinthe raged. *You've betrayed me!* One should not be angry with the Goddess, but she was, oh, she was. One by one, everything she had believed to be true had vanished. She sailed alone beneath a million shouting, spiraling stars, with no lighthouse to guide her.

Chapter Twenty-four

In Daine Miekel's class the next day, Cerinthe gripped the pianoforte and worked doggedly at the barre exercises. She had slept poorly, dreaming that she was a wounded bird flailing on the ocean, struggling after the Sea Maid in the distance. A hundred sea monsters rose from the deep and coughed with a hundred different voices: You have no passion, you have no soul. Cerinthe tried to gather the fragments of the scallop bowl floating on the waves. She begged the Sea Maid to return, begged her to sing, but the Sea Maid sailed away until only a strand of her red hair streamed out along the blue horizon.

"An excellent développé, Cerinthe," Daine Miekel said as he passed her.

Cerinthe bit her lip. Was he merely being kind because he had heard what happened at the rehearsal? She forced her développé higher and pointed her toe so hard it cramped. She commanded her body to do her will, trying to feel nothing, fighting to ignore the words that pounded like a bittie-bom drum: "I have become what someone else wanted me to be…."

In front of Cerinthe, where the pianoforte belled out at the base, Elliana plopped her leg into a développé in seconde and admired herself in the mirror. She forgot to point her toe. Cerinthe hated every knobby bone of Elliana's flexible spine. Blast that white swan! Cerinthe wished she'd throttled it before it had the chance to sway the priestess.

"Elliana Nautilus!" Daine Miekel exclaimed. Dawson stopped playing. The class stopped dancing.

"Yes?" asked Elliana, startled.

"I have had enough!" The daine scowled, his sleek, cat-like body tense. "Your feet look like flopping bedroom slippers. Your turnout does not exist."

Two bright spots burned on Elliana's cheekbones. Cerinthe smiled to herself.

"You are throwing away a great gift," Daine Miekel said, pacing. "It sickens me! Nothing I say or do gets through your vain head. I even placed Cerinthe beside you because she knows how to work. But have you learned anything from her? No!"

Dumbfounded, Cerinthe felt her smile fade.

"Cerinthe has made more progress in the last five months than you have made in two years. Learn to work as hard as she does before it's too late." The daine shook his finger. "Nemaree doesn't waste her gifts on those who do not seize them. Do you understand?"

Elliana said nothing.

"No? Well, maybe this will help. From now on, Cerinthe will work alone at the pianoforte, and she will lead group one. You are no longer first in this class, Elliana."

The girls broke into whispers.

"Now go to the barre," the daine ordered, "and stand beside Maiga."

Elliana clutched the pianoforte as if she might fall down without it. As she stared at Cerinthe, Elliana's face was so lacking in expression, her eyes so hollow and empty and frozen, that it could have been the face of a corpse. She looked as she had in Kasakol's room when she sat desolate with her scarred, bleeding feet.

Daine Miekel tapped his foot. "I said now, Elliana."

She walked rigidly, a princess of wood, trailing one hand along the pianoforte for as long as she could. Instead of going to the barre, she headed for the door.

"If you go out that door," the daine said, "you don't come back."

Elliana stopped. Her left hand reached over her shoulder, patting, probing, feeling for something on her back. Then she went to the barre, and the girls shifted to make room.

"Quiet down, everyone," Daine Miekel said. "Begin the développé combination over."

After class, Cerinthe stayed to stretch, fuming because the daine had only placed her at the pianoforte to teach Elliana a lesson. Given that, how could she feel any joy in her promotion to first place? For the third time now, including the princess part, she had been used to teach Elliana a lesson. Cerinthe slid into a split and bent forward until her hamstring burned.

On the other side of the studio, Elliana's friends clustered around her. Their voices rose and fell, their heads occasionally turning toward Cerinthe. At last Elliana led them all across the room. Isalette rushed over to Cerinthe and blocked their path, her arms folded over her chest.

"Get out of my way!" Elliana said.

"When the moon turns gold," Isalette said.

"Let her talk all she wants, Isalette." Cerinthe shrugged. "There's nothing more she can do to me. Do you like being second best, Elliana? Beaten by a smudge?"

"Gloat all you want," Elliana said. "You may have deceived the daine, but I assure you, you have deceived no one else. Let me be the first to tell you the good news. Daina Odonna has given the princess part to Maiga." Maiga was Cerinthe's understudy.

"They fitted me for the costume today," said Maiga. "I'm surprised your dear friend here didn't tell you. Miss Chunk was there too, having the bodice on her rose costume let out—again."

"Isalette?" Cerinthe looked up at her.

Isalette hesitated, then nodded.

One at a time, Cerinthe drew her legs beneath her.

Elliana laughed. "I knew the moment I saw your big, coarse hands and your mannish shoulders that you were no dancer. And you never will be. You have no spark, no passion. You don't even have a soul. But I wouldn't worry; you can always get a position as a smudge."

"Stoven and sunk!" Cerinthe leaped up. "I don't believe a word you say. I've had enough of you too. Enough of your jealousy, your lies, and your mean dirty tricks. Tayla is really sick because of you."

Elliana's eyes widened in mock innocence. "Why, then there is an opening in the laundry. How fortunate for you." She sneered. "I could have told Daina Odonna that you couldn't imagine being a princess. When you did those fouettés yesterday, you looked like a drunken fishwife."

"I can do fouettés better than you any day," Cerinthe said.

"Indeed? Are you willing to prove such a preposterous claim?"

"Yes."

"Marvelous! Then let's have a contest. The first one to stop turning loses."

"Fine." Cerinthe stalked toward the center of the room.

"Oh, but not here."

Puzzled, Cerinthe turned. "Where?"

Elliana smiled. "On Kasakol's Gable."

No one spoke. Cerinthe realized she had walked straight into another of Elliana's traps. There's nothing more she can do to me, Cerinthe had said, but now, knowing Elliana, looking at Elliana—all fire and icy menace—she was not so certain. Why compete on Kasakol's Gable? Did Elliana really believe she would become the most brilliant artist of her time if she danced there and won a competition? Elliana was desperate, and Kasakol had always been her guide, her hope, her... Cerinthe's hands curled...her Goddess.

Cerinthe closed her eyes, felt herself falling through a black void. Into it surged a tide of anger, and she wanted to rip the barres from the walls, wield them like giant clubs, and smash the windows and mirrors and pianoforte. Then she saw herself standing lost in the rubble.

"She's too scared to dance on the Gable," Maiga said.

Cerinthe opened her eyes. Why shouldn't she do it? At the very least, maybe Kasakol's spirit would help her with *Archipelago Princess*—the Sea Maid certainly wouldn't. Cerinthe pictured the Gable as she had seen it from the Wind-Rose Room, weighing the danger. Done correctly, fouettés stayed in one spot.

"Cerinthe Gale can't face the ultimate test of who is better," Elliana said quietly. "A test of passion. Not judged by teachers but by Kasakol herself." And she turned to leave.

"When should I meet you?" Cerinthe asked.

Elliana turned back. "In thirty minutes."

"I'll be there."

"Cerinthe," Isalette said, "you can't risk…"

"Yes, I can," Cerinthe said and walked away.

Twenty minutes later, she and Isalette crept up the final attic stair.

"I'm no stickler for rules myself," Isalette whispered. "But the school forbids this for a good reason. A girl died from dancing on the Gable."

"I know," Cerinthe whispered back. "But I doubt if she grew up dancing and playing on cliffs. I'm used to heights."

"They could expel you for this." Isalette shook her head as Cerinthe opened the door that led to the roof.

The sky, half cloudy, splashed above them. To the south, Cerinthe could see the green bluff of Healer's Hill, but the domes and towers of the city hid the sea. Everything looked unreal, like a painting. They crawled over the roof until they reached Kasakol's Gable, where Elliana and her friends were already waiting. Cerinthe immediately saw why.

Elliana stood in the safest spot. The narrow, flat space beside the gable stretched about ten feet across. At the front edge, the drop plunged five stories down to the courtyard. At the back edge, there was also a drop but only to another flat stretch of roof six feet below. Elliana had chosen the back edge. Cerinthe shrugged, put on her dancing slippers, and walked over to the front edge, hearing the slate rasp against her slippers. The wind blew steadily.

"Ready?" asked Elliana coolly. "The first one who stops loses."

"Ready." Cerinthe did not look at the drop. A sudden sense of the foolishness of this crept through her anger, a sense that everything was happening just as Elliana had planned. More girls, pearls, and even some aggies, were crowding onto the roof; word must have spread.

"But if they're both dancing on the Gable," an aggie asked, "which one will become the greatest artist in the kingdom? The legend says only one can be best."

"One of them is bound to fall," said another girl. "Kasakol will see to it."

Elliana's eyes glittered. "Kasakol will help me. Now—"

"Wait," Isalette interrupted. "If either of you touches or crowds the other, you lose instantly and the contest ends."

"Agreed," Cerinthe said.

"Of course." Elliana stared. "This is real. Now, Maiga, give the preparation."

"Are you sure about this?" asked Maiga.

"I said, give the preparation!"

Maiga took a deep breath. "Ready? Second, fourth…and!"

Cerinthe did a pirouette, a plié, and extended her leg to first position, then rose to her toe and spun as her leg whipped out to second position and back into a pirouette again. She repeated this over and over, up and down in one spot on one toe. She never forgot that she was only three feet from a long, and undoubtedly fatal, fall. And she never forgot her anger. With every turn her list of grievances mounted.

I nearly missed getting into the school because of her.

She called me dirty and dingy, a slattern, a drunken fishwife.

She smashed Mama's seagull.

She stole The Dance of the Sea Maid.

Worst of all, she hurt Tayla. Cerinthe spun faster. Elliana spun faster too, matching her. Cerinthe turned faster yet.

Liar.

Thief.

Desecrater…

Her calf ached, but the memory of Tayla's coughs gave her strength. For once, being a commoner helped; she was stronger and stockier than Elliana. On and on they turned. Was it five minutes? Ten? Cerinthe began to gulp air. Her muscles burned, and her supporting leg shook. She was moving around too much. The drop, the drop, remember the drop. She knew she should quit, but refused to yield.

A scream shattered her concentration. She stopped, exhausted and dizzy, and looked toward Elliana.

Elliana wasn't there.

All of the girls were screaming, shrieking, jumping up and down on the dangerous slate. Cerinthe ran to the back edge of the Gable and looked down.

Six feet below, Elliana sprawled on the roof top. She lay on her back, with her left leg horribly twisted. The ragged edge of her shinbone thrust through the skin. From a gash on her right thigh, bright red blood spurted like a fountain.

Chapter Twenty-five

High on Kasakol's Gable, Cerinthe stared at Elliana's blood. It was a bright and vibrant red; blood that pulsed from an artery; blood that flowed directly from the heart. Cerinthe knew that without help Elliana would bleed to death in minutes. Yet, her dancing slippers seemed fastened to the slate. The wind chilled the sweat on her skin, and she shivered. Dobbie's burnt finger flashed before her eyes; Sileree's dull skin; and last, Tayla's flushed face. Cerinthe had not helped them. Why help Elliana, who had caused her so much pain?

She dug her nails against the bandage on her palm while a deeper question, a truer question, pounded like a hammer against her ribs. What if she did help and then Elliana died as a result?

Cerinthe saw her mother's body lying in Gwimma's

dispensary. Though she had watched and watched for her mother's chest to rise, no breath would ever fill her lungs again. In all the room the only sound had been Cerinthe's own breath, smelling the stink, smelling the glimroot. She had hated her breath then, wanted to tear each rib from her body and break it against the wall.

Now, on the Gable, Cerinthe grasped her side. The shaking in her hands shot up through her arms until she jerked her head back and forth. No, no!

The wind blasted like a slap, and Cerinthe remembered where she was. No one else could reach the roof in time, not Mistress Blythe, not Gwimma, not Mederi Grace. Elliana might die from Cerinthe's help, but she would certainly die without it. Again, as on Normost, Cerinthe was alone to make decisions that might bring the Black Ship swooping down. Even now she sensed its presence, and knew if she could glimpse the ocean, she would see the black sails swollen with that terrible, uncanny wind.

No! It wasn't fair! She had stopped healing so she would never have to face this again. She looked across the roof, desperate to escape this dreadful choice. But beyond the roof, beyond all the towers and spires of Faranor, the sheer, green face of Healer's Hill rose inexorably in the distance.

Elliana moaned. Only a moment had passed. Her left hand lay with the palm facing up. Her fingers twitched, and her hand lifted a few inches, reaching toward the sky. As Cerinthe stared at the fragile white wrist, a sound like distant bells rang inside her—bright as sunlight, mysterious as moonlight. It pealed louder and louder, surging past the black fear until finally every beat of Cerinthe's heart clamored in her ears. Then Elliana's hand fell back.

Cerinthe sat down and swung herself over the edge of the upper roof. First she had to stop the bleeding; she knew how to do that. She dropped on the lower roof, avoiding the sharp, jutting slate that had cut Elliana, and knelt beside her.

The blood shot out from above Elliana's right knee, where the femoral artery had been severed. Cerinthe pushed on the pressure point by the groin to constrict the flow. With her other hand, she ripped off a piece of her tunic skirt and scrunched it into a pad.

"Hold this against the wound," Cerinthe said to Isalette, who had climbed down too. Still bearing down on the pressure point, Cerinthe fumbled to untie the ribbons on her dancing slipper. Blasted, blasted knot…

Elliana rolled her head.

"Lie still," Cerinthe told her.

The other girls watched like statues along the upper roofline.

"Maiga," Cerinthe called. "Find Mistress Blythe." But Maiga only stood, horror-stricken. "In Nemaree's name," Cerinthe shouted, "Go! And Jasel, tell the doorman to send for Mederi Grace. Hurry."

Blood soaked through the pad; the pressure point was not enough. Cerinthe took Isalette's free hand and guided it to the point.

"Press there," she said. Isalette's face whitened.

Cerinthe yanked off her slipper. After wrapping the pink

ribbons around Elliana's thigh, she looped them around the slipper, which she then used for a lever to hold the tourniquet. She turned it slightly.

"Kasakol!" Elliana whispered, then went limp. Her eyes shut.

Up above, some of the girls began to sob; others began wailing the death dirge.

"Stop it!" shouted Cerinthe. She squeezed Elliana's shoulder. "I won't let it take you. Do you hear? I won't. Not this time."

Isalette glanced up. "Let what take her?"

Without answering, Cerinthe checked beneath the pad. The bleeding had slowed—thank the Sea Maid.

"Hold the slipper here, Isalette," Cerinthe said. "Don't tighten or loosen it unless I tell you."

Next, she examined the broken shinbone. In spite of the horrible, jagged edges, only a little blood trickled down— nothing life-threatening. Elliana's skin felt clammy though, and her breath raced; she was in shock. Shock could kill.

"Throw me a shawl," Cerinthe called to the girls. "Sylva, Bessor, I need a flask of proturra from the dispensary. It's on the fourth shelf. Below it are some splints and bandages. Bring those too—oh, and a blanket." The girls clambered away.

As Cerinthe draped the shawl over Elliana, she wondered how they could possibly carry her over the dangerous roof. She wiped her forehead against her arm, smearing the blood on her face. Spatters of red stained her royal blue tunic. She felt light-headed, as if the blood were her own, as if she were floating far above the accident. An odd sense of certainty and peace filled her, buoyed by the fierce clamoring that rang on in her head.

Perhaps she was ignorant. Perhaps everything she was doing

was wrong. Nevertheless, she knew this was exactly what she had to do. For as long as she could, she would keep the Black Ship at bay. She would hold onto life, the shell that held the soul up to the light.

Cerinthe looked back at Elliana. What else could be done?

"Ritoria," she called. "Find some cobwebs. There should be plenty up here."

"Cob…webs?" Ritoria squealed between sobs.

"Cobwebs. They help staunch the wound."

Cerinthe elevated the undamaged leg on a stack of slate but feared to move the broken one. She looked doubtfully at the tourniquet. How much longer could she leave it on before causing permanent damage? Without blood, the tissue below would die. For the moment, though, Elliana's ankle still felt warm.

Cerinthe stared over the rooftop at Healer's Hill. There was nothing more she could do. Where was Mederi Grace? Why didn't someone come? She picked up Elliana's hand, touched it with her inner wrist, and willed with all her soul: *Live, Elliana, live.*

Suddenly, someone did come. Cerinthe looked up. Softly, softly on the wind, she heard the Sea Maid sing.

Two hours later, Cerinthe slumped at the table in the dispensary and dropped her head in her arms. Elliana was still alive—barely. Mederi Grace and her assistants had strapped her to a litter and lowered her through Kasakol's unbarred window. From there, they had taken her to the dispensary. Cerinthe had huddled in a corner, dazed, watching the mederi prepare Elliana for the journey to Healer's Hill. A specially equipped carriage waited in the courtyard.

Afterward, too dirty and exhausted to go upstairs, Cerinthe had bathed in the dispensary washroom. Now, as she cradled her head in her arms, the soft blue robe she wore cushioned her cheek. Her hair lay damp against her neck.

Cerinthe sat up and spread her fingers wide. Although her hands looked clean, with the cuticles scrubbed almost raw, she felt that Elliana's blood had soaked into her skin and would never come out.

In the side room, Tayla coughed three times. Mederi Grace had examined her briefly and left instructions for Mistress Blythe; nearly the same instructions, Cerinthe had noted, that Gwimma might have given.

The door opened. Mistress Blythe whisked in with a tea tray in her hands.

"You're looking better," she said, setting the tray on the table. "You were quite a sight, you know." She opened a blue-and-white jar of stemhips and added two pinches to the teapot.

"Who's that for?" Cerinthe asked, suspicious.

"You. Mederi Grace's orders."

"But that will make me sleep for twelve hours!"

"Exactly, dear."

"I can't. I have rehearsal tonight."

"No, you don't. Mistress Krissel has sent a note to Daina Odonna explaining Mederi Grace's orders."

"But I've been doing so poorly," Cerinthe protested. She

rubbed her calf, aching now from the fouettés. "Elliana said they've taken my part away."

"Surely you didn't believe her? Besides, I've heard nothing of it."

"But if I don't go, they're certain to give the part to Maiga."

"Nonsense," Mistress Blythe said briskly. "You're in no condition to dance. You're exhausted, which isn't surprising." She sat down across the table. "I shudder to think what would have happened if you hadn't shown such presence of mind. The mederi said Elliana would have bled to death."

"I was afraid I'd do something wrong," Cerinthe said.

"Well you didn't. Mederi Grace said you showed good judgment and great imagination in the way you handled the entire crisis."

"She did?" Cerinthe asked, sitting straighter. Mistress Blythe nodded, then poured the steeped tea and handed her the cup. Cerinthe took a sip. Warmth spread out inside her, and it wasn't only from the tea.

"Did the mederi say," Cerinthe began, "whether Elliana will be able to dance again?"

"It's too soon to know. Her leg…" Mistress Blythe sighed. "She will get the best possible care, you can be sure of that. I only hope her parents will visit her."

"Why wouldn't they?"

"Lady and Lord Nautilus are not very affectionate parents, I'm afraid. Elliana's been rather neglected."

"But isn't she rich?"

"Oh, she's had all the pleasures and governesses that money can buy, but she receives no attention from her parents."

Mistress Blythe smoothed her collar. "You see, Elliana grew up in the shadow of her six older sisters, the famous Nautilus Beauties. Unlike her, they are not terribly intelligent girls. The only attention she received was what she could obtain from mischief—and as you know, she excels at that."

Cerinthe nodded.

"Later, when her extraordinary talent was discovered, Elliana became special; dancing gave her a place in the world. I believe she wants to be a dancer solely for the attention."

"Partly," Cerinthe said. "But Elliana is a true dancer. In her soul, I mean."

Mistress Blythe looked startled. "Then without her dancing, Elliana will be lost."

Lost…lost…the word seemed to echo through the dispensary—bouncing from the bookshelf to the blue-and-white porcelain jars, flying from the doorlatch to the windowpanes, and ricocheting from one brass pan on the scale to the other. Cerinthe looked down at the table.

"Mistress Blythe," she said slowly, "we should never have danced on Kasakol's Gable."

"No dear, it was very foolish."

"I should have said no when she dared me! I should have walked away. I've always managed to ignore her before." Cerinthe paused, clicking her nails on the saucer. "Will we be expelled?"

Mistress Blythe patted Cerinthe's cheek. "If it were up to me, I would say no. You've both paid a heavy price. But it's not up to me. I only hope this incident finally dispels that ridiculous legend about Kasakol. Now, you drink that up and lie down in the room next to Tayla's where I can keep an eye on you."

Cerinthe swallowed the last of the tea and soon her eyelids drooped. After she lay down, the accident replayed in her mind. She tried to recapture the absolute certainty, the peace, the fierce roaring that had tingled through her body, and most of all, the elation she had felt when the Sea Maid sang.

A breath of wind blew in from the open window. Cerinthe turned over, facing it, unwilling to sleep, clinging to the good feelings as if she were trying to eat the same chocolate again and again. She had helped Elliana and she hadn't died...helped and hadn't died; shown great imagination; the Sea Maid sang...she sang...and she sang!

Chapter Twenty-six

Each day following the accident, Cerinthe woke full of joy, expecting to hear the Sea Maid's voice again. Her room, the school, the theatre—everything seemed to glow with color. She danced better, slept better; even the oyster stew tasted better. Then, as the days passed and the Sea Maid remained silent, the joy vanished, leaving Cerinthe more desolate than before.

On the eighth day, after Cerinthe had badgered her endlessly, Mistress Krissel allowed her to go to Healer's Hill and visit Elliana. With all the last-minute preparations for *Archipelago Princess*, no one could be spared to accompany her.

"Stay on the main road," Mistress Krissel warned. "It's safer. And don't speak to anyone. I don't know why I'm making an exception for you." She wagged her finger. "You don't deserve it, though you did save her life. Now get on with you. Be back in three hours, or I'll think up a punishment that no one has even heard of yet."

Wrapped in her royal blue cloak like a protective shroud, Cerinthe walked alone through the city. She barely noticed the shops or the bustle of people and vendors until a huge sign in a dressmaker's window caught her eye:

Exquixite Gowns For
Archipelago Princess *Gala*

She pressed her nose against the cold glass and felt her stomach cramp. Daina Odonna had not taken the princess part away. During the final rehearsal yesterday, Cerinthe had danced the solo from beginning to end without interruption. Tomorrow night, hundreds of people would be watching her, a former smudge, pretend to be a princess.

"I don't care," she said and plodded down the street.

After twenty minutes, she reached the bottom of Healer's Hill, where the towers, buildings, and formal landscapes of the city ended. Ancient oaks soared to the sky. Shrubs and wild flowers grew where they willed. A road wound up the hill, but not far away was another route: a flight of stone steps beneath a canopy of red camellias.

Cerinthe hesitated. Stay on the main road, she remembered. It's safer. She chose the steps, climbing up and up until even her strong dancer's legs began to burn. The hill was higher and steeper than it had looked from Majesty Bay. When she was far above the city, she paused to look down. To the north, a spring squall swept over the bay, misting the shipyards. She wondered what Thordon was doing. Why hadn't he answered her letters?

She sighed and climbed on. Gradually, the roar of the sea increased. *Sea Maid*, Cerinthe prayed, *where are You?* Sunlight brushed the yellow lilacs that drooped over the steps. At last the stairs crested the hill and flattened into a flagstone path. After a few more steps, she emerged from the trees.

There, across a green lawn, a three-story building sat in the lee of the hill. Cerinthe blinked; the sun reflected brightly off the white exterior walls and the rows of windows. She wanted to laugh, thinking of all the terrible tales the folk told about the mederi's schools—dark places where evil magic secrets passed from hand to hand.

At the front door, a boy greeted her and bowed; his short muslin robe swung out over his buff trousers. He glanced at the crest on her cloak.

"I've come to visit Elliana Nautilus," Cerinthe said.

"She's Mederi Grace's patient," he said, after checking a list. "You'll have to ask her permission. If you like, I'll take you to her."

"Thanks," Cerinthe said.

"My name is Vruce of Baywater."

"I'm Cerinthe Gale of Normost."

His eyebrows raised. "Then you're the one who..." he stopped.

"Who what?"

"We've heard about you," is all Vruce would say. Cerinthe wondered what he had heard.

Vruce led her into the building, up one flight of stairs and down a hallway. Plain white walls stretched up from the varnished oak floors, rubbed to a golden glow. A few serene pictures hung on one wall. Benches of dark polished walnut sat against the white expanse, and light from the tall windows made a haze of brightness. Cerinthe wanted to sit on one of those benches for hours and hours; sit, sink down, and think of nothing.

Some of the people they passed in the hall wore muslin robes, either short ones like Vruce wore or long ones like Mederi Grace wore. Perhaps the muslin robe was a uniform, though the style varied from person to person. Cerinthe shifted her shoulders, feeling conspicuous in her grand cloak.

"What kind of job do you have here?" she asked Vruce.

"I'm a second-year apprentice. Next year I'll be assisting patients," he added proudly.

Apprentice to the mederi! Cerinthe looked at him in awe. "Is it true that the mederi have magical healing powers?" she asked. "Is that what they teach you?"

"Magical powers?" Vruce pushed out his lower lip. "I suppose some people might call it that. We do learn about the power of healing with our minds and spirits, but that's only part of it. They also teach us how to diagnose and treat illness and injury using herbalism, surgery, proper food, and body manipulation techniques." He rattled them off without pausing. "We learn from observation, books, experimentation, and dissection as well as from mental and spiritual exercises."

"Oh," Cerinthe said, startled.

They found Mederi Grace reading in the library. Vruce left.

"I'm glad to see you," Mederi Grace said, smiling. "I wanted to speak with you the last time we met. However, as you know, I was in rather a rush."

Cerinthe was looking around the room, filled with shelf after shelf of gleaming books.

"Are all of these books about healing?" she asked, astonished. She thought of *Leigh's Herbal* and all she had learned from only one book. Think what she might learn from hundreds!

"They're about healing and herbalism, physiology, surgery, metaphysics, the study of the mind, and the mysteries of the soul." Mederi Grace laughed. "That's all."

"My Gwimma doesn't think that healing can be learned from books."

"I see. Is she a folk healer?"

"Yes."

"Unfortunately," Mederi Grace said, "people often fear and mistrust what they don't understand. Did she teach you the skills you used with Elliana?"

Cerinthe nodded.

"Then you're a folk healer too."

"Not anymore," Cerinthe said, looking away. "I've come to visit Elliana. May she have visitors?"

"Yes, but about your healing—"

"I don't have much time," Cerinthe interrupted. "*Archipelago Princess* is tomorrow, you know. Can I see Elliana now?"

Surprised, Mederi Grace leaned back in her chair. Cerinthe curled her fingers and, without thinking, dragged her nails across her unbandaged palm.

"Ouch!" she said, then cursed herself.

Mederi Grace seized Cerinthe's hand. She looked down at the raw open sore, then looked sharply up at Cerinthe.

"It's nothing." Cerinthe pulled her hand away, disgusted because her voice sounded small. "Please. I'd really like to see Elliana now."

In the silence, Mederi Grace watched her. It seemed to Cerinthe that the mederi noticed every little thing but not in the critical way that Daina Odonna did.

A moment later, the mederi nodded. "As you wish," she said.

She led Cerinthe out of the library and up a flight of stairs to another floor, where more people walked through the halls. A few wore muslin robes. Others, dressed like servants, carried trays of food, or hefted basins of water, or wheeled carts in and out of the sickroom doors. No one wore black.

Each door had a paper placard listing the names of the patients inside. When Mederi Grace reached a door with Elliana's name—with only Elliana's name—she stopped.

"After you've finished your visit," she said, "have someone show you to my study. I need to treat your hand. And we need to have a chat."

Cerinthe stared at the swash on the N in Nautilus and nodded, although she knew she would not go. She could guess what the mederi wanted to discuss.

The mederi knocked on the door, then opened it and put her head inside. "A visitor for you, Elliana."

"Mother!" Cerinthe heard Elliana exclaim. "At last! Why didn't you come yesterday? You promised you would, directly after Lady Skya's brunch!"

With the mederi following, Cerinthe walked into a bright,

airy room. Elliana turned toward her eagerly, then puckered her forehead.

"You!" she said. "What are you doing here?" Elliana lay propped up in bed, covered with an orange quilt that made her red hair look dull. Purple shadows circled her eyes. Wires and pulleys and suspended weights elevated her leg, which was encased in a cast from ankle to hip. An empty blue pitcher shone on the bedside table. On the tablecloth, a wet stain spread from the mouth of an overturned glass. Behind it, was a drooping bouquet of hothouse flowers—lilies, roses, iris.

"I've come to visit," Cerinthe said slowly, unnerved by Elliana's glare. "Are you feeling better?"

"How dare you come here?" Elliana pulled the quilt to her chin. "I am expecting my parents at any moment. If they find you here, they will have you thrown into prison."

Cerinthe's mouth fell open. "What…do you mean?"

"This, fool." Elliana jabbed one finger at her suspended leg. "This was all your fault. Luring me out onto Kasakol's Gable. And everything you did with that stupid ribbon hurt me even more. I've no feeling in my leg now. How dare you touch me with your filthy, common hands?"

Cerinthe stepped back.

Elliana hit the bed. "How dare you!"

"Elliana!" Mederi Grace said.

Her eyes frantic now, Elliana leaned toward Cerinthe. "You crippled me!"

Cerinthe clapped one hand to her mouth, fighting a surge of nausea. No. It couldn't be true. In Nemaree's name, let it not be true!

"You crippled me because you're jealous," Elliana shouted. "You knew that you would never dance as well as I do. You wanted to destroy me so I'd never dance again!" She seized the vase, and hurled it at Cerinthe, who ducked. "You and that cursed Kasakol!" The vase shattered. "After all I did for her. Believed in her!"

"Stop this!" Mederi Grace rushed to restrain Elliana's thrashing. "You'll undo all we've done!"

"But I'll show you!" Elliana screamed, her face red and contorted. "I'll show you all! I won't let them cut it off! I won't! I will dance again! Now get out! Get her out of my room!"

Chapter Twenty-seven

Cerinthe ran out of Elliana's room, down the hall, and down the stairs—lily petals and iris buds scattering from her cloak. After two flights, she burst out a back door. Across the lawn, at the top of a rise, an old hawthorn hedge snaked away in both directions. A white arbour in the middle framed an open gateway. Cerinthe raced toward it, darted through, and stopped on the other side.

Elliana crippled! Her leg to be amputated! The tall firs above Cerinthe seemed to lean in, menacing and careening, as if about to topple down and crush her.

"What did I do this time?" She pounded on the arbour, shaking the wild, white roses that climbed up the sides and cascaded over the top. Had she left the tourniquet on too long? Had she neglected the broken leg? She had stood frozen on Kasakol's Gable, uncertain whether to help, fearing something like this would happen. And it had. It was her mother and the glimroot all over again. Again Cerinthe had used her healing skills, and again disaster had resulted.

"Mama!" she cried. "I shouldn't have done it! I shouldn't have done it!"

Pictures flashed through her head. She saw her mother wading knee-deep in the surf, scooping up a crab with a swift swing of the net. She saw Elliana dancing the Sea Maid's dance as beautifully as if she were the Sea Maid Herself. Then Cerinthe saw herself: raising the knife over her mother's bloated leg; wrapping the ribbons around Elliana's bloody thigh. One of them would never breathe again. The other would never dance again. What would Elliana have—what would she be—without her dancing?

"I should have let the Black Ship take her!" Cerinthe sobbed into her cloak.

Had this happened because she was jealous? Was Elliana right? Cerinthe knew she had been jealous and angry, too, over the sacrilege, the blackmail, the Goddess's partiality, Tayla—so many things. But she had never, never meant to cripple Elliana. She had meant to help. Hadn't she? Or had she been so swollen with hatred that—

Footsteps crunched on the path behind her.

"I am sorry," Mederi Grace said. "I didn't realize."

Sobbing harder, Cerinthe turned away.

"You must understand," the mederi said. "Elliana is in a state of emotional shock."

Cerinthe dropped the cloak and whirled around. "But it's happened again!" she cried. "Don't you see? It's just like before. She said you have to…cut off her leg!"

The mederi grasped Cerinthe's shoulders. "No. That's not true."

"But she hasn't any feeling in her leg and—"

"Please. I want you to take a deep breath."

Cerinthe took a long, shuddering one.

"That's better." Mederi Grace let go of her. "Now, if you stay calm, I will explain Elliana's condition."

Cerinthe nodded.

"First, Elliana is exaggerating because she's depressed. To her, everything seems hopeless; that's a normal response for this stage of recovery. She has sensation and a strong pulse in her broken leg. The wound in her thigh caused serious tissue damage, but it will heal. She won't lose either leg, and she will walk again—all thanks to your skill and quick-mindedness."

"But walking isn't enough," Cerinthe said, wiping her eyes. "Not for Elliana. Will she dance again?"

Mederi Grace hesitated. The top of the arbour curved over her head, and she seemed crowned with roses and thorns.

"The bone-setting and surgery went well," she said at last. "With time, using all the arts of healing that we know, Elliana may dance again. But there's no certainty." She reached into her pocket and handed Cerinthe a handkerchief. "A lot depends on Elliana."

"But she'll be so far behind."

"Yes. And that's why Daina Odonna believes there may be a blessing in this accident."

"A blessing?" Cerinthe asked. "How?"

"The daina said that although Elliana is extraordinarily

gifted, she has seldom worked. So her gift is no longer developing." Mederi Grace wove her fingers through her braid. "Those who ignore the Goddess's gifts usually lose them. To overcome her injuries, Elliana will have to work as she has never worked before. That tantrum may be the first sign of new motivation."

"If she did work," Cerinthe said, "Elliana could be…her picture would hang in the Gallery of the Great some day."

"Exactly."

A breeze brought the smell of mint, and Cerinthe glanced around. Her headlong flight had taken her into a garden where plants flourished in long, raised beds.

"The herb garden?" she asked.

Mederi Grace nodded. "We grow whatever medicinal plants we can cultivate. But we grow flowers too—for the patients." She pulled a weed from a bed of yesta. "If you like, I'll give you a tour."

Cerinthe followed her down a brick path half overgrown with moss. Magenta and gold poppies bent in the wind. Lavender, clover, and the faintest suggestion of ramalon— pungent and sweet—scented the air. Cerinthe recognized old friends—hyssop, lemon balm, and yarrow, as well as other plants she knew from the *Herbal.* All of them seemed to be thriving.

At the end of the garden, a seedling sprouted from a cedar stump the size of a well. Mederi Grace stopped beside it and pointed up the path, which led on through the trees.

"There's a spectacular view of the sea from the top of the bluff," she said. "It's one of the highest spots on the island."

Cerinthe felt tired and sat down on the stump. She could see each ring in the wood, all the years of the tree's life until the axe had come for it. The tight, dark knot in the center seemed like the pain that crouched in her chest.

Mederi Grace turned toward her. "You said something like this had happened before. And I remember how frightened you were when I opened the jar of glimroot. I suspected then you were a folk healer. Only healers use glimroot and only as a last resort."

Cerinthe plucked a leaf with five pointed spikes from a bush. As she rolled it between her fingers, sharp pops of apple filled the air. What was its name? What was its use? What was its being? And what was hers?

"That is called tirsal," Mederi Grace said. She paused. "Will you tell me what happened?"

Cerinthe looked up into her eyes; they had golden brown flecks the same color as her skin. The braid that hung over her shoulder looked as thick as a rope, a rope you could climb, a rope you could trust with your life.

"I found a piece of metal on the beach...." Cerinthe began. She told the story, leaving out only the Sea Maid and the Black Ship. As she talked, the pain grew sharper.

"Perhaps the glimroot did kill her," Mederi Grace said when Cerinthe finished. "However, from the symptoms you describe, I think your mother would have died anyway. You had to try everything—everything you knew or guessed or dreamed. You had nothing to lose. I think you showed tremendous courage."

"But if I'd known the right cure—"

"Sometimes there isn't one." Mederi Grace stood silently, watching the white clouds chase across the sky. "You see, a mederi heals by reaching inside and drawing forth every part of herself: her knowledge of the lore, her experience, her understanding of the particular patient. She uses her passion and imagination and, most important, her connection with the divine. To heal someone, a mederi combines all of these in a creative way. That's why healing is an art as well as a science."

Mederi Grace smiled, and her joy seemed to embrace not only Cerinthe but also the garden, the hill, the island—even the sky.

"You have demonstrated many of these qualities, Cerinthe," she said. "Demonstrated them so well, in fact, that I invite you to come to Healer's Hill and train to be a mederi."

"Me!" Cerinthe exclaimed. "A mederi?" A spark leaped inside her, as though these were the words she had been waiting to hear all of her life. After one shining moment, though, the spark flickered and died. She banged her heel against the stump. "But I don't have imagination or passion—Daina Odonna said so. She said I have 'a failure of the soul.'"

Mederi Grace stiffened. "When did she say that?"

"During a rehearsal."

With her lips pressed together, the mederi turned away. Her muslin robe flared, then fell back in soft, sinuous drapes.

Cerinthe dropped the tirsal. Now the mederi would not want her to come. She did not know whether to feel relieved or disappointed.

"I must say I disagree." Mederi Grace turned back, her eyes shining fiercely. "Only the Goddess knows another person's soul. You have passion, Cerinthe. You have imagination. And what you did for Elliana—and your mother—proves that you have considerable healing ability."

Cerinthe shook her head. "Even with everything I learned from Gwimma, I still couldn't save Mama." She paused. "From what I read in *Leigh's Herbal* though, Gwimma doesn't know very much. If I had been a mederi, could I have saved Mama?"

Mederi Grace held out her hands. "There's no way to know for certain. Even a mederi might have lost her."

Lost her, lost her... Cerinthe pressed her hand against her heart.

"Does your chest hurt?" Mederi Grace asked.

"It aches. Sometimes there's a sharp, stabbing pain."

"When did this start?"

"After I came to Faranor."

Mederi Grace studied her. "Any coughing? Ankle swelling? Shortness of breath?"

"No, none."

"Good. Tell me, if this pain could speak, what would it say?"

Cerinthe closed her eyes. Somewhere in the garden, a crow squawked, chiding, jeering—on and on and on.

"I saw the Black Ship," she whispered, "coming to take Mama away. All because of my mistake. No matter what I did, I couldn't stop it. I never want to make it come for someone else. I never want to see it again—until it comes for me."

There was a silence.

"Now I understand," said Mederi Grace gently.

Out on the edge of the bluff, the wind gusted hard, bending the boughs on the firs; yet, as they had for hundreds of years, the trees withstood the onslaught. The wind blew the mederi's robe backwards until it shaped her body like a white spindle flame.

"Death is strong," she said. "I, too, have seen the Black Ship. But this I believe: The ship is black only because our vision is too weak to see what it really is. Why else would Nemaree send silver dolphins swimming beside it?"

"You lose patients?" Cerinthe asked, then blotted her tears.

"All mederi do. But our failures are less important than our willingness to try to help. More than passion, more than imagination and skill, the urge to help is the most important quality for a healer. That urge comes from love."

"But I didn't help Dobbie when his finger was burned," Cerinthe said. "Or help Sileree with her sore throat. And Tayla, when she lay so sick with pneumonia, I didn't help her."

"I believe you wanted to," Mederi Grace said. "You feared hurting them, though, feared bringing the Black Ship. But on Kasakol's Gable, when it mattered most, you mastered your fear and did everything in your power to help Elliana.

"If you come to Healer's Hill," she added, "we will help you understand visions like the Black Ship, so they will aid rather than overwhelm you. Such visions come to those with the potential to be mederi. You will learn the way to the power inside yourself. That is the 'magic' that so many fear."

Cerinthe gave the handkerchief back.

"I am astounded by your story," Mederi Grace said, "by all you accomplished alone with your mother and with Elliana. The Goddess has given you a remarkable gift."

A gift? Cerinthe felt light-headed. A mederi, she thought again. Me?

"But I've always dreamed of being a dancer," she said slowly. "Healing was only something I did; like eating, drinking, and sleeping."

"It's a difficult decision," Mederi Grace said. "Think it over carefully. What are you in the deepest place inside your heart? What do you feel the most joy doing? And when you feel that joy, what speaks to you or through you?"

Cerinthe thought of the Sea Maid's voice and the bright, mysterious bells that had rung deep inside her on Kasakol's Gable. Then she thought of her dancing, *Archipelago Princess*, and her mother urging her to be a great artist. Her fingers curled over the edge of the stump, probing the ridges and crevices in the bark. She had already made her choice. Hadn't she?

Chapter Twenty-eight

At eight o'clock the next evening, the curtain rose on the long-awaited performance of *Archipelago Princess*. Up in the gilt-encrusted royal box, Princess Zandora herself sat between Queen and King Seaborne. The theatre was packed.

Cerinthe walked to the wings and waited for the triumphant Naming Day scene to end. Her stomach flopped like a halibut in the hold of a boat. Her pink silk costume swished as she ground her slippers in the resin box. How smooth the silk felt, how different from rough muslin. Before she had left Healer's Hill, Cerinthe had asked why the mederi wore muslin.

"It's easy to wash," Mederi Grace had said. "And, because we consider ourselves servants of our art, we dress simply." Cerinthe had yet to decide between dancing or healing—or even to wonder if she had a decision to make at all—because of the flurry over the ballet.

The music changed. Cerinthe swallowed hard, stepped near the edge of the scenery, and took her preparatory position.

Sileree, wearing a grown-up version of Cerinthe's pink silk costume, stood in the wings across the stage while two seamstresses took frantic tucks in her bodice. She had grown thinner. When her eyes met Cerinthe's, she nodded, but her face seemed lifeless and sad.

Cerinthe thought of another sad person; Elliana lying forlorn—or more likely throwing a tantrum—up on Healer's Hill. Not only had she lost the princess part she coveted, but she had also lost the rose part in Act Two. Only a few weeks ago, Cerinthe would have felt delighted instead of sorry. Elliana would have been the perfect princess, as Juna had said.

Wait…Cerinthe lifted her chin. That was it! While she danced, she would pretend she was Elliana. Although Cerinthe didn't know any real princesses, she knew "Her Highness," Elliana Nautilus, quite well. Cerinthe smiled. Why hadn't she thought of this before? She would dance as if she were the most exquisite, extraordinary girl in the kingdom.

Her music began. The viols frolicked; the flutes trilled; and the harps rippled the silly melody. Cerinthe held out her skirts and pranced onto the stage. She danced like a princess, a rather spoiled, arrogant princess. When she finished her solo with the dizzying burst of piqué turns and came back into the wings, Daina Lizabrina hugged her.

"Wonderful!" the daina exclaimed. Cerinthe blushed and then ran to change into her rose costume for the next act.

After Princess Zandora's sixteenth birthday party in Act Four, the ballet ended. The blue velvet curtains swept shut, then opened again as applause rang through the theatre. Footmen began lighting candles in the sconces on the walls. The entire cast crowded onstage, the principal dancers in front. Everyone bowed. Then, one at a time, Daina Carroll and the other principals took separate bows. Last of all, Sileree and Cerinthe—who had changed back into her princess costume—clasped hands and ran to the front of the stage.

Hundreds of people rose to their feet. They clapped. They shouted and cheered. "Vox! Gale! Vox! Gale!" The royal family waved, their crowns glittering, their jewels flashing.

Cerinthe curtsied again and again. Stoven and sunk! she thought, the audience liked me! Me, Cerinthe Gale of Normost, a commoner! If only her mother could see her now. A steward of the royal house presented each of the girls with a bouquet of pink hothouse roses.

Later, still in costume, both girls attended Princess Zandora's reception in the immense ballroom above the theatre. Her Highness had requested that they be presented to her. Cerinthe was dazzled by the swirling gowns—the purple satins, white velvets, and gold embroidered silks; dazzled by the polished parquet floor; dazzled by the crystal chandeliers that blazed with so many candles they seemed to outnumber the stars. As if she were a small child again, Cerinthe tucked her hand into Sileree's.

"Sileree, my darling!" Daina Odonna cried, walking up with Daine Rexall. "You were charming! Beautiful!" She tossed a kiss from her fingertips. "I am so pleased." She twirled the stem of a fluted glass; the red wine looked brilliant against her black velvet gown. Around her throat was a diamond-studded collar. "What a special addition Sileree will be to the company next fall," she said, turning toward the daine. "Don't you agree, Rexall?"

"Indeed. Special addition. Quite so."

Sileree nodded politely. Her cheekbones looked sharp, her face gaunt. She seemed more exhausted than usual, but the daina, busy chattering and sipping her wine, did not seem to notice.

Finally, the daina spoke to Cerinthe. "Well, Cerinthe Gale, all our hard work was worthwhile, was it not? You were the perfect little princess tonight, child. You performed just as I wanted you to. I shall forge an artist out of you one day, as I have Sileree."

Sileree stiffened and dropped Cerinthe's hand.

"Thank you, Daina," Cerinthe said. She, too, nodded politely but clenched her hands behind her back. Did she now have a soul? Passion? Imagination? Had Daina Odonna bestowed them upon her? How very kind. The daina really knew nothing about her at all, not the way Mederi Grace did.

A royal steward approached them. He bowed, and tiny blue pom-poms bounced on the edge of his jacket.

"Her Royal Highness will receive you now," he said.

Cerinthe and Sileree glanced at each other, then followed him while the daina and daine trailed behind. They passed beneath the gallery where the musicians played. They passed a long table laid with silver, crystal, and delicate gold-edge china that looked as if it might snap under the weight of a single grape. Cerinthe could not believe she was an honored guest in such a place. This was exactly the kind of life her mother had imagined for her.

When they reached the far end of the ballroom, the steward spoke to the crowd, and the people parted. On a foot-high platform, the royal family sat in golden chairs upholstered with blue velvet. The queen was whispering to the king from behind her painted fan. Princess Zandora leaned forward and smiled at the girls.

The steward spoke. "Your Majesties, Your Royal Highness. May I present Sileree Vox of Umbrea and Cerinthe Gale of Normost."

Trying not to tremble, Cerinthe stepped forward beside Sileree and curtsied low. The queen and king inclined their heads. Princess Zandora rose and stepped off the platform, her train dragging behind her. White lace trimmed her turquoise dress, like froth on a blue wave.

"I want to thank you both," she said, "for your lovely dancing. What a wonderful birthday present you have given me. And I have a little present for each of you—so that you will always remember my gratitude and this night." As she turned, her orange coral necklace swung sideways.

Cerinthe watched her, surprised; the princess did not seem arrogant at all. Although she lacked Elliana's beauty, the princess had the high cheekbones and green eyes of the Faranor nobility. Like Cerinthe and Sileree, she had dark blonde hair. A pair of gold-rimmed spectacles perched on her nose. Cerinthe thought Daine Rexall's interpretation of her was quite wrong. Rather than waltzing through the grand palace hallways as a child, she had probably curled up in some cushioned corner with a book.

A page knelt before the princess. He held a blue pillow with golden tassels; on it lay two black velvet boxes. A pair of diamond earrings glittered in each box.

"Please accept these as a small token of my esteem," Princess Zandora said. When neither girl moved, the princess lifted the boxes and gave one to each of them.

"Thank you, Your Highness," Sileree said.

"Yes, thank you very much, Your Highness," Cerinthe half whispered.

"It is I who thank you," the princess said. Then she grinned. "I must confess that I was never so graceful as either of you. Please tell me, is there anything else I may do to express my gratitude?"

"No, Your Highness," Sileree said. "Thank you."

Cerinthe didn't speak; a wild idea was filling her mind.

The princess smiled at her. "And you, Cerinthe Gale of Normost, is there something you wish?"

Cerinthe hesitated, then the words rushed out. "Yes, Your Highness, there is."

Startled, Sileree looked at her. A few people coughed delicately. A grizzled man, standing behind the king, fingered a medal on his chest and murmured. The queen lowered her fan. Only Princess Zandora showed no surprise.

"I asked you because I truly wished to know," she said. "And it is something that is, perhaps, important to you?"

Cerinthe nodded.

"Then please do me the honor of telling me what it is."

Cerinthe took a deep breath. "Sometimes the students or servants at the royal school get sick or injured. No one with proper training is there to care for them right away, so they get worse. These earrings are beautiful, but…" She held out the box. "Please, would you sell them and use the money to get a healer or mederi for us? That's what I wish."

The group around the platform grew ominously silent. The pages, courtiers, and even the steward gaped. When Princess Zandora turned toward the queen, Cerinthe's heart pounded.

Then the queen spoke. "You may approach us, Cerinthe Gale of Normost."

Terrified, Cerinthe stepped toward Queen Endorian Dorthea Mistral of the Royal House of Seaborne, the Queen of all Windward, and curtsied to the floor.

"You may rise." The queen wore loops and loops of pearls. They began just below her chin and circled tightly around her throat, covering every inch. From there, each strand drooped lower across her bosom until the longest one touched her lap. She twisted her fingers through one of the strands; it clicked.

"Are your words true?" the queen asked. "The School of the Royal Dancers, under our patronage…" She glanced at one of the royal ministers standing nearby and the pearls clicked faster, "…has neither a healer nor a mederi?"

"Yes, Your Majesty." Cerinthe's voice was a squeak.

"We did not know. We are extremely grateful to you for bringing this matter to our notice." The queen nodded at Princess Zandora.

The princess turned back to Cerinthe. "Although we appreciate your gracious offer to use the earrings to help your fellow students, it is not necessary. Please keep them and remember me and this birthday that you have helped to make so lovely."

Cerinthe stammered her thanks, curtsied again, backed up a few steps, and turned away. She and Sileree were halfway across the ballroom when Daina Odonna swooped down on them.

"Cerinthe Gale!" she exclaimed, her black eyes raging. "How dare you embarrass me in that manner! And worse yet, you have humiliated Her Majesty! You owe the queen everything, down to the clothes on your back! I will deal with you later." And she stalked away.

"I don't care what you think," Cerinthe said. "It's more important that the school gets a healer." Then, startled by her own boldness, she glanced up at Sileree and saw her smiling. It was the first time Cerinthe had seen her smile—offstage— in weeks.

"You have more courage than a crow's nest watcher during a storm," Sileree said. "Good for you." She touched one of the earrings in the black box. Cerinthe looked down at her own.

Eight lozenge-shaped diamonds formed petals around another diamond. The earrings were quaint and delicate and exactly like Sileree's. Cerinthe had never dreamed of owning anything like them. How pleased her mother would have been.

"I didn't expect a gift," Sileree said. "They're worth a bit. But not enough to…" she snapped the box shut, her face bleak and still again.

After the reception, back at the school, Cerinthe rushed to the dispensary to show Tayla the earrings and tell her about the performance. Tayla was asleep, however, so Cerinthe went to bed.

All night long, the pink hothouse roses sat beside the earrings on her bedside table, where the seagull had once stood. She breathed the heavy, intoxicating scent. In her dreams, lengths of white muslin and pink silk tangled together. They scattered white petals that floated away on the sea and drifted toward black sails in the distance.

Mederi Rayden came to work in the school dispensary the next day. After examining Tayla, he pronounced her well enough to travel and sent her to recover in the country. She could never work in a laundry again because her lungs were too weak. When Cerinthe told him how the smudges lived, the mederi dropped a pair of scissors, which clanked onto the floor.

"Conditions like that in this day and age?" he asked, his smooth, round face puckering like a raisin. "In the queen's institution? Show me."

Cerinthe took him below stairs, and he groaned when he saw the sniffling girls wading across the cold, wet floor. He ordered many changes, much to the vexation of Mistresses Odue and Dalyrimple and to the delight of Mistress Blythe.

Now that Tayla was safe and *Archipelago Princess* was over, the events of the last few weeks struck Cerinthe hard. Night after night she lay awake, thinking of the choice that lay before her: dancing or healing? Daina or mederi? In spite of her anger at the Sea Maid, Cerinthe prayed to Her for help, but the Sea Maid continued Her silence.

"Cerinthe, pay attention!" Daine Miekel exclaimed several times in class. "Did playing the princess go to your head?" But Cerinthe couldn't pay attention. Each time she did an exercise, she wondered if it would be the last. By Saturday, she could bear it no longer. She slipped down to Majesty Bay, sat down beside Old Skolla, and told him the whole story.

"And Mederi Grace asked me to come to Healer's Hill and be an apprentice," Cerinthe finished. "But I don't know what to do."

Old Skolla whistled. "She would not ask lightly. Many people apply to be apprentices on the hill." He was carving a piece of walnut; his wrinkled hands looked as dark and grainy as the wood.

"Then why are there so few mederi?" she asked.

"The training's hard. Few are chosen. And fewer yet complete the apprenticeship. Most earn only the title of healer."

"But I've always dreamed of becoming a great dancer. I've learned so much, worked so hard."

"Prevailing winds change, little daina." Old Skolla leaned back against the stone wall, his eyes keen. "Sometimes you weigh anchor. Sometimes you choose to come about. You think you've reached your destination, only to find it's not your final harbor, merely passage to another. Look." He held out the piece of roughly carved walnut. "What will this be?"

"I see a wing," Cerinthe said. "No—maybe a fin?"

Old Skolla squinted. "At first a skylark seemed waiting in the wood. So my knife carved, seeking that shape. But soon a different shape called to me, a dolphin—and after all that work on the skylark." He clicked his tongue. "To seek the new shape, Old Skolla had to let the old one go."

Cerinthe frowned. "What if the new shape isn't as good as the old one?"

"Aye, it would've been a good skylark, that's certain," he said. "But if the skylark stays, the dolphin's lost—or never found. So which would you rather? A good skylark forced upon the wood or a dolphin that sings out from the soul of the grain?" He tapped his thumb against the walnut. "The wood will guide you to its truth—if you let it, little daina, if you hear it. Find the truth in the wood and you'll find the greatness; toss all else to the wind.

"And if the dolphin fails…" Old Skolla shrugged, "…well, no mortal controls the winds of the world. And this wood will always feed the fire."

Cerinthe sighed and looked out at the bay, where the morning mist had never cleared. One by one, the clouds huddled together, threatening rain.

"But what will everyone say?" she asked. "Daina Odonna, Daine Miekel, my father, Tayla, and Gwimma? Elliana? If I quit dancing, they'll all think I'm a failure." And what would her mother have said?

"A failure! Who could say so," he scoffed. "Not when you have danced before the queen herself! Besides, all that matters is what your own heart says. True success is measured here."

He thumped his chest. "Spoken here."

He began carving again. "A shame Old Skolla did not see you dance."

"You didn't go!" Cerinthe exclaimed. She had been given one ticket for *Archipelago Princess*. When Tayla had been too sick and Thordon—her second choice—had never written back, she sent the ticket to Old Skolla. "But why didn't you go?" she asked him.

He slapped his left leg. "Because this doesn't take me far— not on roads two feet can travel." And he hitched up his robe.

Cerinthe gasped. From his thigh to his foot, Old Skolla's entire leg was made of wood. A series of pegs allowed the knee to bend or straighten. He had carved the wood with ships under sail, with dolphins leaping over crescent moons, and with blooming flowers—she recognized camellias and daisies and waterlilies. Vines spiraled around Nemaree in her forms as Fish Goddess, Snake Woman, and the six-breasted Great Creator.

"I didn't know," Cerinthe said. She had never seen Old Skolla walk or even stand.

He dropped the robe. "It's of small matter."

"Small matter! But how?…"

"An accident aboard ship. Terrible storm off the Raven's Teeth. Cleaved the thing off quick as a wink."

Cerinthe squeezed her eyes shut, but alarming images swarmed in her mind, and she opened them again.

"It ended my seafaring days," Old Skolla said, "and began my carving days." A thin shaving curled from his knife and fluttered away. "As for your ballet, Old Skolla thought it best to give his ticket to one whose legs are stronger." He arched one craggy eyebrow. "And here he comes."

Cerinthe looked up. Thordon was walking toward them with his hands stuffed in his pockets. As usual, his head bent slightly forward as if he were fighting the wind.

"You gave your ticket to Thordon!" Cerinthe exclaimed.

"Aye. The lad comes every Saturday, after the yards get out at noon, on the chance he might see you. Or, lacking that, to have a bit of talk with an old sailor."

"I never knew," Cerinthe said. "I thought he didn't—" and then Thordon was there.

"Hello," he said, his blue eyes shining at her. She stood up, uncertain whether to fling her arms around him or march away with her chin held high.

"Now off with you both," Old Skolla said, waving his hand. "You're interfering with trade."

Thordon walked silently toward the center of the market, and Cerinthe followed. She could not believe that he had been coming every Saturday.

"Thordon…" she blurted.

"Cerinthe…" he began.

They laughed—a short, uneasy laugh that broke off awkwardly.

"You first," he said.

"Why didn't you answer my letters? After that argument we had?"

"Because I couldn't say what I wanted to say—not in a letter."

"Then you still want to be friends?"

Thordon looked at her. "Would I be here otherwise?" He jerked one hand from his pocket and the gray flannel turned inside out, scattering lint, crumbs, and a strip of dried fish with teeth-marks on the edges. "You don't understand, do you?" he added. "You didn't then and you don't now."

"Then for the sea's sake," she said, "tell me what's wrong!"

"All right. Remember how I talked about the New Western Isles? Told you I wanted to join the colony once I'm a shipwright?"

She nodded.

"I hoped maybe you'd come too." Thordon walked faster. "I thought, when the time comes, we could get married."

Cerinthe stopped directly in front of a huckster's tent.

"See the incredible beast!" the huckster shouted, scenting a customer. "See it change from a cat to a shark in the blink of an eye. Only three shellnars a peep for you, little lady!"

"Get married?" Cerinthe said to Thordon. Then he did care for her, he truly did.

"Yes. But the colony won't need any…" Thordon scratched his neck.

"…any dancers," she finished for him. "There won't be a company there for years. Or even a school."

"No. And when you got such a big part, I realized how good you must be. I knew then you'd never want to leave."

"See it now!" The huckster waved his orange hat. "Cat to a shark! Blink of an eye!"

Cerinthe moved away. They started walking again.

"After seeing you in the ballet the other night," Thordon

said, "I know that you belong here. You're sure to get into that company some day."

"Thanks," Cerinthe said slowly, remembering the glitter of the theatre, the cheers, the elegant reception, and the excitement of being presented to Princess Zandora. Then she looked up at Healer's Hill. Today the top was lost in the low-lying clouds. "What are you in the deepest place inside your heart?" Mederi Grace had asked. "Success is measured here," Old Skolla had pointed to his chest. Cerinthe sighed. Who was she? What did she want to do? What was the truth in the wood?

Thordon smiled, but it seemed grudging. "When you danced, you looked just like a princess."

Cerinthe curled her hand.

"I hardly recognized you," he added. "You belong with all those refined folks." He glanced down at his patched pants. "I've decided it's the right thing for you."

"Storm and thunder!" Cerinthe exclaimed. "Don't tell me what's right for me, Thordon Tycliff! I can choose for myself!"

"I didn't mean—"

"Yes, you did," Cerinthe said. "If I want to go to the colony, I will. If I want to dance, I will. And if I want to be a med..." she stopped, her head tilting. Mederi would be needed in the new colony, as they were throughout the kingdom—particularly in the Reaches. What would it be like to travel among the folk in the Northern Reach, to travel and work as a mederi but one of their own? Could she change their distrust of the mederi?

Thordon was staring at her as though she had turned into a limpet.

"The truth is," Cerinthe told him, "I don't know where

I belong or what I should do." She paused. "There's a woman named Mederi Grace. She has offered to take me as an apprentice."

Thordon seized her arm. "A mederi!"

"I know what you're thinking, but everything we were taught about them is wrong. Here on Faranor, people honor the mederi. She's one of the finest women I know."

"Then she has cast a spell on you!"

"No." Cerinthe pulled her arm away. "It doesn't work like that. What worries me is that I'd have to quit dancing. I couldn't do both."

"Quit dancing? You mean, you would?"

"Hard to imagine, I know."

They had reached the heart of the market district. "Almost gone! Almost gone!" shouted a woman pushing a cart with trays of candied nuts. A baker's boy cast an anxious glance at the glowering sky. "Loaf-end special!" he yelled. "Last of the day!"

"You can't quit dancing," Thordon said. "Think of all those people cheering you the other night. Think what you'd be throwing away, a certain future, money—"

"Don't you think I know that?" Cerinthe cried. "Why do I have to choose? I hate this! What if I make the wrong choice? How come to be one thing you have to give up everything else?"

"Wait a minute." Thordon stopped walking. "I thought dancing was the most important thing to you in the world. Your *dream*?"

"It—"

"Here I was, all ready to give you up and let you have your

dream. Now I find out that you'll quit dancing to be a mederi, but you won't quit to be with me."

Startled, Cerinthe stood silently; she could not deny it. Hot fingers of guilt prickled her face.

"Well, I won't let you become a mederi." Thordon slammed his fist against a barrel. "You can't. I'll stop you."

Cerinthe stepped back. Suddenly she saw him, really saw him, for the first time—his angry red face; his lopsided collar, misshapen because he forced it upward; his hard, square jaw; his jacket with its padding that made his shoulders and arms look bigger than they were.

"I'll write to your father," Thordon said, scowling. "You know how he feels about the bloody spell-weavers. He'll be back on the next ship and make you marry me. You'll never be a mederi."

Without saying a word, Cerinthe turned and left him. She shoved her way through the crowd, bumping a juggler whose pins crashed onto the street and went rolling away. She was furious with Thordon but more furious with herself for failing to see the truth sooner. From the beginning, he had told her what to do—what he wanted her to do. Each time they met he had grown more domineering: "Tell your father to get a job in the shipyard…you're not going to dance forever…once you're old enough to get married, you'll quit…I won't let you become a mederi." To protect his own dreams, Thordon had pretended these things were best for her.

"Stop trying to make me into something I'm not!" Cerinthe shouted to the world. No one noticed, because the rain began hurtling down, and the vendors threw sheets over their wares and closed up early. She did not bother to raise her hood. A sodden throng of people and animals pushed through the streets. In the school courtyard, Cerinthe stopped to watch the rain drip down the faces of the bronze dancers.

Was it her mother who had convinced her to be a dancer, or was it her own choice? And if she became a healer, would it be Mederi Grace who had convinced her, or would it be her own choice?

Cerinthe bowed her head. In the name of the Sea Maid, how was she to know the difference?

Drenched, she slipped into a side entrance and climbed the stairs to the fifth floor to ask Sileree's advice; she was the one person who might understand. Cerinthe walked down the hall until she came to the diamonds' wing. There were only ten diamonds, which meant each girl shared a room with only one other.

"Please no!" Cerinthe heard someone cry. "It can't be true. Nemaree, let it not be true!"

Cerinthe hurried toward the sound and stopped beside an open door. Inside the room, Juna lay sobbing on her bed. The other bed was empty, the white cover smooth, perfectly smooth. Outside, the rain beat against the windowpanes, and the sky darkened toward night.

"Juna," Cerinthe said. "What's wrong?"

Wild-eyed, Juna looked up.

"Oh Cerinthe," she cried. "Sileree is dead."

Chapter Thirty

The next day, during the memorial ceremony in the Royal Theatre, Cerinthe huddled in her seat. Isalette sobbed beside her. All of the students and most of the staff and company were crying too. Sileree Vox of Umbrea had taken her own life—she had deliberately walked into the sea until it closed over her head.

Cerinthe did not weep, nor did she bother to seek the Sea Maid among the painted figures on the ceiling. Her fingernails dug into the plush velvet arm rest, digging and scratching until she wore off the pile. She stared stonily at Daina Odonna up on the stage.

"Sileree was an exquisite dancer," the daina was saying, "her death is a tragic waste, a terrible loss to us all. I shall never understand why she threw away such a promising future." The daina seemed piqued. She looked as immaculately groomed as ever, with her bun smooth and her face powdered, but her hand kept opening and closing over her ruby pendant; it sparkled and went black, sparkled and went black.

Cerinthe wanted to leap up and scream: Why didn't you see the shadows around Sileree's eyes? Why didn't you see how still she was? How thin and sad she was? Why didn't you do something! But instead of screaming, Cerinthe crouched deeper in her chair. She had seen. She had known—and done nothing.

After the service, Cerinthe fled to the dispensary. Mederi Rayden was still in the theatre, administering to some students who had fainted. Cerinthe shut the door and sagged against it, relieved to be alone. Across the room, on the mahogany counter, the sunlight flashed on one of the silver pans hanging from the scale.

Cerinthe walked over and stood in the sun. She remembered the night Sileree had come to the dispensary, when she had said in her sore, beautiful voice: "Don't ever wish to be like me." And later, out in the courtyard: "I wanted to be a singer. I have become what someone else wanted me to be. And now I'm trapped, I'm trapped...."

"I can't feel the sun!" Cerinthe sobbed. She fell to her knees. She yanked out the pearl comb, shook her hair loose, and raked it forward until it hung over her face. *Sea Maid*, she prayed, rocking back and forth. *I need You. Where are You?* Cold crept through the floor and into her uniform, into her bones, into the heart of the pain in her chest. With an icy blast, the Black Ship towered in her mind, so close she could hear the creak of its rigging and the hiss of its wake.

"Go away!" she cried. But the power of the dead pulled her

toward the Black Ship, where specters crowded the deck, jammed the portholes, and covered the skull figurehead looming over the prow. A hundred hands reached out for her. Her body seemed bound with iron; she could not move.

Something glinted off the starboard bow. It scampered; it glimmered and spread, sending trills of light across the dark water. All at once, seven dolphins broke through the swells. Thunder cracked as light blazed from their silver bodies and turned the sea around the ship a sparkling, sapphire blue. The dolphins leapt and plunged, cavorting by death's side. Or were they death?

"The ship is black only because our vision is too weak to see what it really is," Mederi Grace had said. "Why else would Nemaree send silver dolphins swimming beside it?"

Their tails were made of diamonds, their fins of pearl. On their heads flashed silver crowns. Each time they jumped, they left white rainbows hanging in the air. Their bodies shone like pewter, then crystal, then opals. In that sea of light, Cerinthe swam closer and closer until she touched one radiant body, touched it and did not die.

But neither did the Black Ship disappear, nor did its stench of death. If anything, against the brilliant blue, its hull looked blacker than before. As Cerinthe shrank back, afraid she might see her mother or Sileree among the dreadful specters, the dolphins vanished and so did everything else.

Cerinthe opened her eyes to find herself still kneeling in the dispensary, with her hair tangled over her face. She took one breath after another, pushing away the horror of the ship, holding close the memory of the dolphins. It seemed impossible to keep the one without the other though, and she let the dolphins fade.

Cerinthe waited, hoping the peace of the dispensary would calm her, but it didn't. When she was little, she had always fled to Gwimma's dispensary for comfort.

Gwimma. Home. Normost—her father. They were all so far away, leagues and leagues away across the sea.

"I'm lost," Cerinthe said. She had been lost since she came to Faranor, no, even before. She had been lost since her mother died. Cerinthe put one hand on the counter and dragged herself up, glancing across the room. On the corner table, back in its old place of honor, was the white, fluted scallop bowl that she had broken. It shone in the sun.

Cerinthe stared, wondering, doubtful, then walked toward the bowl. Was this another vision? But fissures crinkled the glass where the fragments had been painstakingly fitted together. She traced them with her fingertip. In one way, the bowl was more beautiful than before, because of the love and care that had gone into making it whole. And it had not so much been mended as remade—transformed. It was the same bowl, and yet it was not.

Cerinthe looked at the fine lines crisscrossing her palms. The sore was still red, though improving daily from the salve Mederi Grace had given her. Healer's hands, the mederi had called them. And in their flesh Cerinthe seemed to hold every person she had ever touched in healing. Her eyes blurred.

"It's too late for Sileree," she said. "I must decide before it's too late for me."

❈

Thirty minutes later, she was running up the stairway to Healer's Hill. The wind blew hard and seemed to be rising. With each step she struggled against a weight that dragged at her feet, a weight that grew stronger the higher she climbed.

"Think of all you'll be giving up," Thordon had said. And her mother, "Be an artist, Cerinthe, a great artist." And Mederi Grace, "Come to Healer's Hill and train to be a mederi." So many voices—where was her own?

Soon the emerald lawn lay before her, and the building where the mederi worked gleamed softly beyond. Cerinthe ran to the hawthorn hedge behind the northern wing. She ran through the arbour, the mass of wild, white roses arching over her head. She ran through the herb garden, past the cedar stump, and on up the hill until she came to a low, weathered fence at the edge of the bluff. There, a seagull piped. As it flew off the fence into the sky, Cerinthe looked out at the sea.

The tide lay at high slack. The wind seemed to be shifting, curling the water into white tendrils. Far out, the fishing boats worked with their downriggers lowered. To the south and west, islands humped like the backs of enormous whales. A scattering of rocky specks dotted the horizon, but these, too, were distant islands. Beyond her sight were even more islands, extending all the way past the Southern Reach where at last Windward ended and the uncharted seas began.

Against the din of the ocean, Cerinthe heard the chime of trickling water. She turned and saw an old fountain tucked beneath the fir trees. A girl—a small, stone figure—knelt in the round pool, her moss-covered face looking toward the sky. One hand was raised as if she had just scooped up the water that overflowed it in a steady stream. Cerinthe pressed the vibrant jade moss, felt it crinkle beneath her fingertips.

A gust blew her hood backward, whipping her unbound hair. She glanced at the ocean and saw, from the direction of the waves, that the wind was barreling from the northwest. Her eyes filled; she had not stood in the northwest wind for six long months. Its fury, its chill, and its old familiar slap against her ears made Cerinthe long for the Goddess even more. If only the Sea Maid would sing, would tell her what to do....

Cerinthe stood, transfixed, as something new occurred to her. Even on Normost, the Goddess had never sung after her mother had died.

"Sea Maid," Cerinthe called. "Did You leave me because I failed with Mama and the glimroot? Then why did You sing again on Kasakol's Gable when..." Suddenly everything that had happened snapped together in her mind.

"You left me because I quit healing!" she cried. She sank down on the rim of the fountain.

On Normost the Sea Maid had sung to Cerinthe not only when she worked in the dispensary but also when she danced, rowed, dug for clams, washed dishes, and at many other times as well. But as soon as Cerinthe had stopped healing, the Sea Maid had stopped singing altogether. She had broken Her silence only once, on Kasakol's Gable, when Cerinthe had used her healing skills to help Elliana.

Cerinthe leaned over the pool. Was healing the link between the Goddess and herself? She remembered the certainty and joy she had felt on the Gable—in spite of her fears. For those minutes she had not been lost but deeply herself.

"The Goddess has given you a remarkable gift," Mederi Grace had said. And when she spoke of Elliana: "Those who do not hear and treasure the Goddess's gifts usually lose them."

Cerinthe shivered. If she accepted this gift, she risked the Black Ship. But if she denied it and the Sea Maid and became a daina instead, she risked a danger just as deadly. Half-sick, Cerinthe blinked at her reflection in the pool; it was flat and still, like a mask.

That danger was silence. The Sea Maid's eternal silence. Equally terrible would be the longing for Her song, the emptiness without it. The fountain without water. The moss brown. Without the Black Ship, there would be no dolphins of light.

Suddenly Cerinthe plunged her hands into the pool, cupped a handful of water, and dashed it up across the moss on the statue's face. The water trickling over the girl turned the moss a deeper green, the stone a deeper grey. Cerinthe threw one handful after another, until waves sloshed along the sides of the fountain, splashing her cloak. She jumped to her feet and turned toward the sea.

"I won't give up Her song!" she shouted. "Not for anyone. Not for anything, not even to keep away the Black Ship. Because Her song is my song!"

The wind roared. Cerinthe felt something coming to her hand, felt something sweeping up from the power in the sea. Her voice emerged from where it had lain hidden from the Black Ship, hidden from the critical eyes and babbling voices. Her voice, but changed, stronger. She seized it. She held it fast.

Her soul was not for the stage, but here on Healer's Hill in the brunt of the northwest wind, it came whole to her hand. Her body burned, fierce with this coming into power.

"This is how I want to feel," she cried. "This is what I want to be. I am a healer. I choose to become a mederi."

From out over the uncharted sea, sweeping in over the rocky specks, tossed by wave after wave until it reached the bluff on Faranor—the Sea Maid's voice came singing. It rang like a bell, but vibrated with undertones that Cerinthe had never heard before; it was whole like the scallop bowl; and it was as pure as the white muslin robes the mederi wore.

It was a voice of love.

Mederi Grace had said that healing was an art.

"Mama," Cerinthe shouted. "Sileree! I will be an artist, a great artist! And I will be myself!" Laughing, she cupped her hands and caught another handful of water from the fountain. There in the northwest wind blasting across Healer's Hill, Cerinthe began to dance; she spun and bright drops of water flew from her hands.